Bob Hartman's Unauthorized Bible Tales

The Unauthorized Version

Now for the other side of the story!

The Bible version of the Old and New Testament tales may be the official one. But there were plenty of characters on the sidelines who saw things from a different angle.

Packed full of humour, mischief, silliness, and fun: these unauthorized versions from master storyteller Bob Hartman get to the heart of the matter.

Bob Hartman knows how to captivate an audience, and regularly entertains children and adults around the world as a performance storyteller. He is perhaps best known for the widely acclaimed *Lion Storyteller Bible*. When he is not writing, Bob enjoys watching films, driving his cars, and entertaining his grandchildren.

Published by Lion Children's Books
an imprint of
Lion Hudson plc
Wilkinson House, Jordan Hill Road,
Oxford OX2 8DR, England
www.lionhudson.com/lionchildrens

ISBN 978 0 7459 6285 6

e-ISBN *Old Testament Tales*
978 0 7459 6725 7 (epub); 978 0 7459 6724 0 (Kindle)
e-ISBN *New Testament Tales*
978 0 7459 6728 8 (epub); 978 0 7459 6727 1 (Kindle)
e-ISBN *More Bible Tales*
978 0 7459 6806 3 (epub and Kindle)

First edition 2016

The stories in this book were first published in *Bob Hartman's Old Testament Tales*,
Bob Hartman's New Testament Tales and *Bob Hartman's More Bible Tales*.

A catalogue record for this book is available from the British Library

Printed and bound in the UK, February 2016, LH26

BOB HARTMAN'S BUMPER Tales from the Bible

THE UNAUTHORIZED VERSION

LION CHILDREN'S

Contents

The New Testament

Introduction

I like the word "bumper".

I'm a bit of a petrolhead – that means I'm crazy about cars! So when I think of "bumper", I naturally think of those things at the front and the back of a car that are the first things you come in contact with if you "bump" up against it. That's how I see this "bumper" edition of Bible stories.

This is an "Unauthorized" version of the Bible. Most of these stories are silly, even stupid, sometimes. They retell the Biblical events in a reasonably accurate fashion, but also play with them. They come from the point of view of sources that were not official or traditional. And they are told by voices that don't necessarily get a hearing in the Bible, including:

- Noah's dog
- The dead boy Jesus raised
- The Health and Safety Inspector at the battle between David and Goliath

They are, in effect, a kind of fun "first contact" with the Bible. My hope is that, if you have bumped into these stories, you might want to take a closer look at the rest of the car, so to speak – at what lies beyond the bumper. At the Bible itself. And God, of course, whose story the Bible tells.

And, yes, I know that the editors meant the other kind of "bumper" when they came up with the title: big, large, like a bumper packet.

But I like to look at things sideways. Bumpers and Bible stories alike. Because when I do, I discover things that I might not have seen if I had let them hit me straight on. And I hope that, having read this Bumper Book, you will feel that way, too!

Bob Hartman

The Old Testament

Adam's Version

The Garden of Eden

"Right then, Adam," God announced. "I've got a job for you to do!"

"A job?" said Adam, lying on his back and sucking on a plum. "What's a job?"

"Erm… it's a task," God replied. "A work-related activity that requires a bit of effort and creativity on your part. Like when I made the world. Though on a much smaller scale."

"Hmm," Adam frowned, sucking the juice off his fingers and tossing the stone on the ground. "Not really sure I'm up for that. Creating stuff, I mean."

"It will be a different kind of creating," God explained. "I'll send animals your way, and all you have to do is make up names for them."

"Oh," said Adam, relieved. "That doesn't sound too difficult. Names for animals? Sure, why not? And you don't mind if I carry on lying here?"

"Not at all," God replied. "Though I suspect that you might find it necessary to move… eventually. Some of the animals are rather large."

"I'll keep that in mind," Adam shrugged, peeling a banana. "When do I start?"

"Immediately," said God. "Oh, and there's one other thing. You might like to keep an eye open for a helper. A companion."

"Got it," said Adam, chewing furiously. "Name the animals. Look for a helper. Anything else?"

"Just a suggestion," God replied. "You're meant to eat the inside of that fruit and throw the outside away. Not the other way round."

"I'll make a point of remembering that," said Adam, spitting out a mouthful of skin. "Ready when you are."

And as soon as he'd said it, a big fluffy creature bounded up to Adam, put its paws on his chest, and started licking his face.

"Enough! Enough!" cried Adam, pushing the animal away and leaping to his feet. Adam was afraid that the animal would be angry, but it just stood there, tongue hanging out and tail wagging. He could have

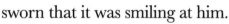

sworn that it was smiling at him.

"Hmm," he muttered. "A name? Let's see. How about 'Happy Licky Waggy Thing'?"

And the animal made a noise. "Woof!"

"I'll take that as a 'yes'," Adam grinned. "Now go away, Happy Licky Waggy Thing. God is going to send me another animal."

But the Happy Licky Waggy Thing just stood there, wagging away.

"All right then," said Adam. "Stay if you'd rather. I don't mind. Maybe you're supposed to be my helper."

So the Happy Licky Waggy Thing stayed and watched with interest as several other animals paraded by.

"Right," said Adam. "I think I'll call you… hmm… 'Fluffy Snuffly Hoppy Thing'."

And the Happy Licky Waggy Thing went "woof" again.

"I'm glad you approve," Adam replied.

And so it went on. He named Snappy Scaly Thrashy Things, Beaky Pecky Clucky Things, Poky Shelly Lumpy Things, and Sting-y Stripy Buzzy Things.

And when God came to visit that evening, Adam was lying on the ground again, exhausted.

"This creating business is hard work," he sighed.

"Tell me about it," God replied. "I needed a rest when I was done. And you've barely started. Oh, and have you found a helper yet?"

"Nah," Adam sighed, struggling with a banana stem. "I thought that Happy Licky Waggy Thing might have been the one, but he's entirely too agreeable. I can't be getting all these names right – but he always acts the same. A wag and a woof. I think I need someone to challenge me. To keep me on my toes."

"Couldn't agree more," said God. "Oh, and there's an easier way to open that. Have a word with that creature above you there, in the tree."

"What? The Cheeky Jumpy Swingy Thing? Sure. Why not?"

So he chucked the banana in the air and the Cheeky Jumpy Swingy Thing grabbed it, turned it upside down, and snapped open the bottom of it with a flick of his thumb.

"Amazing!" thought Adam. "Perhaps that's supposed to be my helper."

The next day was much the same. Adam named the animals, and the Happy Licky Waggy Thing woofed his approval. But the Cheeky Jumpy Swingy Thing was much harder to please. In fact, he screeched and chattered and shook his head at every one of Adam's suggestions.

"Growly Roary Tawny Thing?" said Adam.
Screech!
"Stinky Blacky Whitey Thing?" he offered.
Chatter!
"Spiky Curly Bally Thing?" he tried.
A shaking of the head!
And when God came to visit that evening, Adam was lying on the ground once more, frustrated AND exhausted.

"There's no pleasing that creature," he muttered, gnawing on the fuzzy shell of a coconut. "And THIS! Are you sure this is food?"

"One problem at a time," God sighed. "No, the Cheeky Jumpy Swingy Thing was not created to be your helper. And, yes, that thing you have in your hands is indeed meant to be eaten. But once again, the foody bit is on the inside."

"And how am I supposed to get at it?" grumbled Adam, banging it against his head.

"Throw it on the path over there… right… now!" said God.

CRUNCH!

So Adam did, just as a Trompy Stompy Trumpety Thing trundled by.

"No! Wait!" cried Adam, as a huge grey foot fell on his food. And then he smiled and said, "Oh yes, I see." And he picked himself up and picked over the pieces and picked out the soft white lumps from inside.

"MMM," Adam chewed. "That's good!"

"I couldn't have put it better myself," God agreed. "But the difficulty you're having getting at all the good food I made for you suggests that you might need that helper sooner rather than later."

"I don't mind looking a bit longer," Adam shrugged. "Actually I found a very nice Milky Moo-ey Patchy Thing today. Could that be my helper?"

"Don't think so," God replied.

"The Quacky Splishy Webby Thing?"

"Again – no."

"How about that Baby Scratchy Meowy Thing?"

"And what help would that be?" asked God.

"Don't know, but it's so cute," grinned Adam. "With its big brown eyes and its cuddly little paws."

"Don't be ridiculous," God sighed. "It'll only grow up into a cat. No, I think your helper needs to be tailor-made. Go to sleep, and in the morning you will find what you have been looking for."

So Adam went to sleep. And while he slept, God took a rib from Adam's side. And out of that rib, God made Adam a helper.

The next morning, Adam named the animals again, with the Happy Licky Waggy Thing on his left side and the Cheeky Jumpy Swingy Thing on the right. "I think we should call that a Longy Stretchy Necky thing," he suggested.

Happy Licky Waggy Thing woofed. Cheeky Jumpy Swingy Thing screeched.

And then a voice from behind them said, "I like the Stretchy Necky bit. But I think the Longy bit is a little repetitive. What about SPOTTY Stretchy Necky Thing?"

"That's not bad," agreed Adam. "Not bad at all."

And then he stopped and a shiver went up his spine. It wasn't God who was talking, and it wasn't one of the animals either. Slowly he turned around. And his animal friends did the same.

Happy Licky Waggy Thing went, "Woof!" Cheeky Jumpy Swingy Thing leaped up and down excitedly.

And Adam just went, "Wow!"

"Excellent name," God chuckled. "And I have the

17

sneaking feeling that generations of men to follow will choose the same one. But I have decided to call her 'Eve'. Adam, meet your helper!"

"Pleased to meet you, Eve." Adam smiled.

"The pleasure is mine." Eve smiled in return.

"Would you like to name some more animals?" asked Adam.

"I'd love to," Eve replied. "But I'm feeling a little hungry. I don't suppose we could eat that thing over there?" she asked, pointing at a melon.

"I've had a bit of a problem with those," Adam confessed. "I've licked them and I've gnawed them, and frankly they don't taste very good."

"Perhaps the foody bit is inside, somehow," Eve suggested, picking up a rock. "What if we whack it and crack it open?"

"I think that might help," Adam nodded. "That's a great idea!"

"I think it might," God agreed. And Eve set about whacking the melon.

"So what do you think of your helper?" God whispered to Adam.

"She's perfect," Adam replied. "Everything is just perfect now."

"Perfect," God mused. "Hmm. That's exactly what I was going to say."

Dog's Version

Noah and the Ark

Dog jumped up and down.

"Fox, Fox!" he woofed. "I need to talk to you. Right now."

Fox stuck a nose out of his hole.

"This doesn't have anything to do with your master's chickens, does it?" he asked, suspiciously.

"No, no! What chickens?" Dog woofed. "But it does have to do with my master."

"Never mind the chickens, then," Fox shrugged, sticking his head out as well. "So tell me about your master, if you must. Though why you insist on remaining in that ridiculous slave relationship escapes me."

"I know, I know!" Dog woofed. "But this time it might help. My master is building a boat. And I saved a seat, just for you!"

Fox pulled his shoulders out of the hole, and propped up his cheek on his paw. Then he chuckled.

"A boat, you say?"

"Yes, yes!" Dog woofed. "A BIG boat!"

Fox smiled a bemused smile. "I have to confess that I have always wanted to ride on a boat. A salty breeze blowing through my fur.
A jaunty sailor's cap on my head. Yes, it sounds like heaven." And then he raised his eyebrows and lowered his voice. "The only problem is that we are miles and miles away from the sea. Has your master thought of that?"

"Yes, yes!" Dog woofed. "He has thought of that. You see, we won't be going to the sea. The sea will be coming to us. Sort of. See?"

Fox sighed. "No, I don't see. And I especially don't see how the sea will be coming to us."

"Sort of," Dog woofed. "I said, 'Sort of.'"

"And how exactly will that happen, then? 'Sort of'?" Fox replied.

"It's going to rain!" Dog woofed. "Rain and rain and rain! And rain."

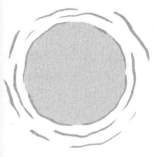

Fox shifted his other paw to his other cheek. "Rain?" he repeated, incredulously. "Rain here? In what most people would call a desert?"

"That's right, that's right!" Dog woofed.

"Rain hard enough to float a boat?"

"A big boat!" Dog woofed. "Very big! Big enough to carry two of every animal in the world!"

Fox tried not to laugh. "I'm working very hard to be polite," he sniggered. "But your master's idea is sounding more and more absurd. A boat big enough to carry two of every animal in the world would have to be enormous, for a start – assuming that you could collect two of every animal in the world. And to float that boat, you would need so much rain that everything we see around us would have to disappear beneath the water."

"I know, I know!" Dog woofed.

"I'm pleased to hear it," Fox replied. "Your loyalty has not blinded you to reason and common sense."

"No, no!" Dog woofed. "I know that it would take an enormous boat. And I know that it would take an even enormous-er flood. But that's what's going to happen. And that's why I'm here. So you can get on the boat and be safe!"

"I'm touched," said Fox. "I truly am. We have had our differences over the years – mostly to do with those chickens – so your concern for my well-being is particularly moving. But I won't be moving, from this spot *or* onto this enormous boat of yours, because your master's idea is, quite frankly, crackers."

"Oh, it wasn't his idea," Dog woofed. "Not his idea at all!"

"That is a relief," Fox sighed. "I was worried, for a moment there, that his insanity might affect you personally. That he would insist on calling you 'Plumcake' or dress you up in children's clothing. So whose idea was it, then?"

"God's!" Dog woofed. "It was God's idea."

Fox rolled his eyes. "Hmm. Well. Yes. I should have guessed."

"So you talk to God, too?" Dog woofed.

"No," Fox sighed. "I do not talk to God, my friend. Because there is no such person."

Dog stopped bouncing up and down. "No such person?" he woofed. "No such person? But my master talks to him all the time."

"Perhaps he does," Fox nodded. "Just as I talked to my imaginary friend, Basil, when I was a cub. But even then I knew that Basil was not real."

"How?" Dog woofed. "How?"

"Well, for a start," Fox replied, "he never talked back."

"Then that's the difference," Dog woofed. "That's the difference! God talks back to my master."

Fox sighed even more deeply. "Your master may think God talks back… Plumcake. But it's all in his imagination. Trust me."

"But God told him how to make the boat," Dog woofed. "How long and how high and how wide. And even what kind of wood to use. He was very specific!"

Fox shifted paws again. "And you don't think he just made it up, on his own?"

"He's never built a boat in his life!" Dog woofed. "But God… God made the whole world and everything in it. So surely he would know how to build a boat!"

"Made the world?" Fox mused. "That would be one explanation I suppose… if there were a God."

"So how do you think we got here?" asked Dog.

Fox shook his head. "Don't know. Not really bothered, actually. Maybe it all happened by chance. But I don't think it was because some Big Person in the Sky just magicked us here."

"Why not?" Dog woofed. "Why not?"

"Because a Big Person in the Sky would probably have done a better job of things," Fox replied. "He would have made chickens without feathers, for a start. That would have saved a lot of gagging."

"You're just being silly," Dog woofed. "Just silly."

"I'm not," said Fox. And he looked very serious. "Apart from your mildly bonkers master – who, I must admit, strikes me as a decent sort of fellow – have you spent much time with any humans lately?"

"Well, I spend time with my master's wife and their three sons and their wives," Dog woofed. "And they are all very nice to me."

"Yes, yes," Fox sighed. "Apart from your wannabe-sailor master and his extended wannabe-sailors family, do you have any other contact with humans?"

"Not so much," Dog woofed. "Not so much."

"Well, I do," Fox

explained. "And even in my relatively short lifespan, I have seen them do the most violent and wicked things to each other. Unspeakably horrible things. Not to mention what they do to animals. And the longer I live, the worse it seems to get. Now what kind of God would make creatures who do things like that?"

Dog scratched his head. And his tail. "Dunno. But that's why he's sending the flood."

Fox crawled up out of his hole and looked Dog right in his dog face.

"GOD is sending the flood? Is that what you're telling me? Or, rather, is that what your master believes?"

"That's what God TOLD him," Dog woofed. "God said that people had got so violent and were doing such awful things to each other that he was sorry he had made them. And that he wanted to start over again."

"By drowning everybody?" Fox's eyebrows were raised again.

"Well, not everybody," Dog woofed. "Not my master, Noah. And not his family either. And not the animals who are on the boat. Like me. And you." And then he whispered, "If you come."

"But why Noah?" Fox asked. "Why does he get special treatment?"

"You said it yourself," Dog woofed, "just a minute ago. He's not like the other humans you know. And I guess God knows that, too."

Fox sat back on his haunches and stared at the ground.

"So what you're saying is that God – assuming there is a God – is going to save the world by destroying it?"

Dog looked at the ground too. "Or maybe he's going to save the world from destroying itself by saving a little piece of it. Just enough to start again with." Then he lifted up his head and looked at Fox. "I was just sort of hoping that you'd be a piece of that little piece."

Fox smiled. "I'm flattered. I really am. But I'm also

a fox. And I don't have to tell you what that means. I trust my brain. I survive on my cleverness. It's reason that counts in my world. And my brain tells me that, nice as you are, you and your master are on a fool's errand. I don't see any harm coming from it – apart from you frightening those who believe in your message. And the possibility, of course, that one of the larger animals you have invited onto your boat might decide that it's a Dinner Cruise and choose you as the main course. No, I think I'll decline your invitation. But do have a wonderful time on your pretend trip, in the pretend rain, sent by your pretend god."

Dog looked sad. Very sad.

"So you're saying no just because you think you're smarter than me?"

Fox cleared his throat. "I'm very sorry, my friend, but yes, I am smarter than you. As are dolphins. And pigs. And several other species. Cats, surely.

"I have outwitted you more times than I can count. We're back to chickens again. So why not trust my judgment in this matter, too?"

"Because I'm not stupid," Dog woofed. "I may not be as clever as you, but I'm using my brain, too. I trust my master. He has never let me down. I know that. And I know that people are getting worse and worse – you said it yourself. That's evidence that there is truth to my master's story. And even though

I can't prove there is a God or that he talked to my master, my master has never done anything crazy before and has never lied to me. So I'm using my brain. And I'm using something else. I'm using what a dog is good at. I'm using my loyalty – my trust in the people who love me. And if they're getting on the boat, then I'm getting on with them."

"Fair enough," said Fox, turning around. "I'll come knock on the door in a few days, shall I? You'll have chickens on board, surely?"

"I don't feel like joking anymore," woofed Dog sadly. "Goodbye, my friend."

Then Fox crawled back into his hole.

And Dog climbed onto the boat.

The Counsellor's Version

The Tower of Babel

The woman and her son walked tentatively into the tent. They looked around, nervously, and finally sat themselves down.

Music was playing softly in the background. Some kind of whistle or pipe, the woman thought.

And then, after a few moments, the counsellor pulled back the tent flap and joined them.

"What seems to be the problem, Mrs… Arphaxad?" he asked, glancing at his clay appointment tablet.

Mrs Arphaxad sighed. "It's Obal, my son, here. We don't seem to be able to communicate anymore."

The counsellor looked at the boy, and Obal just grunted, lowered his shaggy head, and rested his chin on his chest.

"And for how long has this been going on?" asked the counsellor.

"Oh, not long at all," said Mrs Arphaxad. "Since just yesterday, in fact – when he turned thirteen."

"I see." The counsellor smiled, leaning back and making a little tent shape with his fingers. "Since he became a teenager, in other words. Well, it's not uncommon, Mrs Arphaxad. I see this a lot. One day – a bright and happy boy. And the next day – well, we can see for ourselves."

Obal grunted and his mum shook her head.

"I don't think it's as simple as that," she

replied. "I think there's more to it. I really do!"

"Raging hormones. Teenage angst. The sudden eruption of spots. I should think that's reason enough, Mrs Arphaxad." And he peeped at his hourglass. "But we do have quite a bit of sand left, if you want to tell me what you think the reason is."

"I think it has to do with something that happened at work," she replied.

"Hmm," nodded the counsellor. "What do you think, Obal?"

And Obal just grunted and shrugged.

"I'm not sure if that's a 'yes' or a 'no'," said the counsellor.

"My problem exactly," Mrs Arphaxad replied. "And it's even worse when he speaks. I can't understand a thing he says!"

The counsellor smiled once more. "Again, not an unusual problem, Mrs Arphaxad. Teenagers have always had their own special phrases. 'Groovy.' 'Slip me some skin.'"

"Yes, well, I think it's more than the odd word," the woman insisted. "As I said, it all seems to have started…"

"At work, yes," the counsellor interrupted. "So you said. So why don't you tell me exactly what happened?" And then he paused, irritated.

"Do you think that music's a little loud?" he asked.

"Now that you mention it, yes." Mrs Arphaxad replied.

So the counsellor reached back and pulled a flap aside.

"A tad quieter, Peleg," he ordered the musician sitting there.

And then he turned his attention back to his clients.

"You were saying…" he continued.

Mrs Arphaxad shifted in her seat, collected herself, and began:

"I run a little mobile snack bar at the big building site on the edge of the city."

"Where they're putting up that new tower?" asked the counsellor.

"That's right," nodded Mrs Arphaxad. "And Obal here comes in and gives me a hand after school. He makes the drinks and does the washing up, and it provides him with a bit of pocket money.

"Well, if I do say so myself, we have built up a bit of a reputation. Bacon rolls in the morning. Freshly prepared sandwiches at lunch. And all our cakes are homemade."

"Sounds very nice," the counsellor noted.

"It is!" smiled Mrs Arphaxad. "So much so, that we had a visit from Mr Shinar himself – the man in charge of building the tower!"

"Very impressive," nodded the counsellor. And

then he held up his hand and pulled back the tent flap again.

"Peleg!" he shouted. "I told you to keep it down!" The counsellor turned back around but the musician just shrugged and kept on playing.

"Musicians," he sighed. "Temperamental. You were saying?"

Mrs Arphaxad leaned forward, grinning. "I was saying that Mr Shinar himself came to visit our little snack bar. Obal made him a lovely cup of tea, and he had one of my cheese scones. Then, when he took the time to compliment me on my cookery skills, I summoned up all my courage and asked him how he thought the tower was going.

"Well, it was like a proper conversation – like he had known me for ages.

" 'Ahh, Mrs Arphaxad,' he said – knew me by name, he did! 'Ahh, Mrs Arphaxad, the tower project is going well beyond all expectations. We intend to make a reputation for ourselves, we do. We're using bricks instead of stone. We're using tar for mortar. Everyone's on the same page. Everyone's speaking the

same language. And, as a result, we believe that this tower will reach right to heaven and give God himself a bit of competition!' "

Mrs Arphaxad leaned forward even further. "To be honest," she whispered, "that last bit did make me a tad nervous. Right up to heaven. Makes you wonder what God would think."

"Well, you'll have to ask a priest about that," the counsellor grinned. "Not really my area, if you know what I mean. But what does any of this have to do with your son's lack of communication?"

"I'm not exactly sure," said Mrs Arphaxad. "It's just that the moment Mr Shinar left, it happened. I turned to Obal and asked him to pass me a butter knife. And he just looked at me, like he hadn't a clue in the world what I was on about. I asked him again – and that's when all the grunting and shrugging started."

"So it happened immediately?" asked the counsellor.

"Just like that," Mrs Arphaxad replied. "It was very strange."

So the counsellor turned again to the boy.

"You need to help us, here, Obal. You really do. I understand how difficult it can be to make that transition from boy to young man. Why, I've been there myself. But you can see how distraught your mother is. Can you give us some tiny clue as to what's going on inside of you, or how we might help?"

And that's when the boy raised his shaggy head. He looked at the counsellor. He looked at his mum. And then, very deliberately, he spoke.

"Iway an'tcay understandway away ingthay ou'reyay ayingsay."

The counsellor looked worried.

"Hmm. Can't make head nor tail of that. I see exactly what you mean." And then he paused. "Mind you, it would help if the music weren't playing and I could hear what was going on!" And he opened the tent flap again.

"For the last time, Peleg!" he shouted. "Could you keep the music down!"

Once again the musician shrugged. But this time, he put down his flute and he spoke.

"Iway an'tcay understandway away ingthay ou'reyay ayingsay."

The counsellor turned white as a sheet.

"Did you hear that?" he cried. "Whatever is going on with your son seems to have affected Peleg as well!"

Mrs Arphaxad put her hands to her face in horror. "You don't suppose it's catching?" she asked.

But Obal was jumping up and down, delighted, and pointing at the musician.

The counsellor pointed as well, first to Peleg and then to his mouth. And then, speaking as loudly as he could, he asked the boy, "DO YOU UNDERSTAND HIM?"

"He's not deaf!" complained Mrs Arphaxad, as the boy kept hopping and nodding and pointing.

"Well, I'm taking it as a 'yes'," replied the counsellor. "And that means we've got some kind of strange language affliction thing going on here. Something well beyond my expertise. I think we need a specialist."

And he opened a different flap and called for his receptionist.

"Miss Joktan, I need you to get in touch with Dr

Hadoram. Immediately."

But the receptionist just stuck her head through the flap, a confused look on her face.

"Que?" she answered. "No comprendo."

"Right then," said the counsellor, leaping from his seat and collecting his things. "Time for me to go now, Mrs Arphaxad. Pleased to have met you. Sorry I couldn't have been more help. All the best to you and your son. Arrivederci!"

And, shocked, he put his hand over his mouth and raced out of the tent and down the street.

Mrs Arphaxad followed, with Obal and Peleg in tow, chatting away to each other.

There was chaos, everywhere. Everyone jibber-jabbering to each other with words they could not understand.

And rising high into the sky, in the middle of it all, stood the tower, half-finished.

Mrs Arphaxad looked up at the tower – and beyond it, to the clouds.

"Competing with God himself?" she wondered. "Hmm…"

Then she turned to her son and gestured, "Let's go." And she waved for him to bring Peleg along as well.

"Might as well get some food into you," she said, pretending to shove something into her mouth.

Obal looked at Peleg. "Eeseychay onesscay," he grinned.

"Umyay!" Peleg replied.

And they headed for their snack bar, in the shadow of the tower, as everyone babbled around them.

The Shepherd Boy's Version

Moses and the Burning Bush

The shepherd boy slumped down beside his bigger shepherd brother. "You'll never guess what I just saw," he said.

"Sheep?" suggested his brother sarcastically.

"No," he replied. "I saw a bush."

The older brother surveyed the barren landscape. "Now that is news," he said, just a fraction less sarcastically. "Perhaps we should tell the sheep. They'd love a nice bush to chomp on."

"It wasn't an ordinary bush," the shepherd boy added.

"A special bush then?" sniggered his brother. "Dripping with honey, was it? Covered in jewels? The sheep will be pleased."

"Stop it!" glared the shepherd boy. "This is serious. The bush was on fire!"

"That is serious," his brother agreed with a smirk. "But not what I'd call special. There is this little thing called lightning, you see…"

"I know about lightning," the shepherd boy sighed. "And there wasn't a cloud in the sky. Anyway, that's not the special thing. The special thing is that the bush was on fire, but the bush wasn't burning up!"

"Really?" said the older brother sceptically.

"I swear! Honest!" said the shepherd boy.

"And you watched this burning, not-burning bush for how long…?"

"For ages!" insisted the shepherd boy. "I couldn't take my eyes off it. And not one of the leaves was burned. I promise."

"Mmm-hmm," nodded the older brother. "I've heard of those bushes. Distantly related to the smouldering dandelion and the heat-resistant hyacinth, I believe."

"It's not funny!" shouted the shepherd boy.

"Oh yes, it is," grinned his brother. "You have no idea." Then he plucked something from the ground. "And look, here's a slightly singed blade of grass. Result!"

"You can laugh all you want," the shepherd boy sulked. "Moses was there and he saw it, too."

"Moses?" replied his brother. "Crotchety old Moses – the shepherd who lives on the other side of the mountain? Mildly Mad Moses who is always mumbling to himself? That Moses?"

"It's just the way he speaks," the shepherd boy muttered.

"Oh, so you've met him then?" asked his older brother. "I didn't realize you'd had the pleasure. You know they say he killed somebody once?"

"I didn't meet him," the shepherd boy explained. "I sort of ran away when he arrived, because, yeah… well… I heard he'd killed somebody once. And I hid behind a boulder."

"Was the boulder on fire, too?" inquired his older brother.

"No! Of course not! Stop it!" shouted the shepherd boy.

The older brother tapped his chin with his forefinger, thinking. "So if you didn't meet Moses," he asked, "how do you know the way he speaks?"

The shepherd boy said nothing for a bit. He just looked at the ground. "If I tell you," he muttered, "you'll think I'm crazy."

"We passed that point some time ago," said his brother. "Try me."

"I know what he sounds like because I heard him…

talking… to… the bush."

"Mildly Mad Moses," the older brother shrugged.
"What did I say? The name fits. Now if YOU had
been talking to the bush, that would have been
different. Or if the bush had talked back…"

The shepherd boy turned his head, looked at his
brother, smiled sheepishly, and raised one eyebrow.

"Please don't tell me that the bush talked back,"
said his brother.

"The bush talked back," whispered the shepherd
boy. "Actually, to be fair, it was the bush that sort

of started the conversation."

"Mmm-hmm," the older brother nodded again. "And what did the bush say? Let me guess. 'Do you have any water? I'm on fire!' maybe. Or 'I could do with a trim.' Put me out of my misery, please! What did the bush say?"

"'Moses'," said the shepherd boy. "It said, 'Moses, Moses.' And when Moses said 'Here I am!', the bush told him to take off his sandals."

"That would not have been my first guess," his brother smirked.

"It's not funny," said the shepherd boy. "It was really scary! I took off my sandals, too, just in case."

"Just in case what?" asked his brother.

"In case the god in the bush got really angry with me."

"Oh, now there's a GOD in the bush?" said his brother. "That explains everything! You were in the presence of some sacred bit of shrubbery. Does this god have a name?"

"Not exactly," said the shepherd boy. "He told Moses that he was the god of Abraham, Isaac, and Jacob."

"Who are…?"

"Moses' ancestors, apparently," the shepherd boy shrugged.

"Never heard of them," his brother shrugged back.

"Well, according to the bush…" the shepherd boy went on.

"Plant life being the obvious go-to source of information about one's ancestors," his brother chuckled.

"According to the GOD in the bush," the shepherd boy continued, "they are the ancestors of the Israelites – some group of people who are slaves in Egypt. And this god is their god, and he spoke from the bush to tell Moses that he had been chosen by the god in the bush to set those people free."

The older brother paused and scratched his head.

"So these people are slaves in Egypt?"

"Yes."

"The greatest empire the world has ever seen."

"Yep."

"And this god wants Moses to set them free?"

"That's right."

"Mildly Mad Moses?"

"Uh-huh."

"Who lives on the other side of the mountain."

"Yup."

"Who is a shepherd just like us?"

"Exactly."

"Who can't put a sentence together without stumbling?"

"Apparently."

Again the shepherd boy's brother paused. And then he spoke. "The bush didn't give off any smoke by any chance, did it? Deprived you of oxygen? Left you slightly confused…?"

"NO!" the shepherd boy insisted. "That is exactly what the bush – the GOD in the bush – said. Why would I make it up? How could I make it up?"

His brother nodded. "You have a point there. So what happened next? I'm curious. How exactly is Moses supposed to set these people free?"

"The god in the bush said he'd help Moses," the shepherd boy explained. "And he showed him how to do these miracles – turning a stick into a

snake, making his hand all horrible and diseased-looking. And there was something about turning Nile water into blood. It was pretty amazing. Oh, and he said something about Moses having a brother who could do all the speaking for him. Sounds like the god had worked it all out."

"Sounds more like Moses is about to get himself killed," the shepherd's brother said. "Doesn't sound very promising to me."

"I wonder," mused the shepherd boy. "I mean, if this god can make a bush burn – and not burn – and do the miracles I saw, maybe he really can set those people free."

His brother shrugged. "I guess we'll just have to wait and see. I do like that bit about Moses' brother, though. They can be very useful, brothers. And hopefully, Moses' brother will be as helpful as I have been."

"You haven't been helpful at all," sighed the shepherd boy. "You've just poked fun at everything I've said."

"Which is what Moses' brother should do, if he has any sense. And then maybe Moses will forget about the bush, or the god in the bush, or whatever it is, and save himself a lot of trouble."

"So should we go and warn him or something?" asked the shepherd boy.

"What? Moses?" replied his brother. "Are you kidding? They say he killed somebody. No, let his own brother sort him out. I say we go home. I might be wrong, but I thought I heard Mum calling for us."

"Really?" said the shepherd boy.

"Sorry," grinned his brother. "My mistake. It was that olive tree over there."

The Donkey's Version

Balaam's Donkey

When my master told me that we had an important visitor staying, I paid no attention. We'd had plenty of important visitors before.

But when he told me who it was and what I was supposed to do, I could hardly contain my excitement.

"Are you sure you want me to take care of her?" I asked. "There are plenty of older servants who would give anything for this chance."

"No," said my master. "You're just a boy, I know, but I think there is much you can learn from this guest. And also," he added, "being young, you are perhaps more – shall we say – open to unusual things. Things that the others would find just a little disturbing."

I have to admit that I was nervous when I first met her. I'd heard that the first few moments with her could be a bit of a shock. Those lips and that tongue forming those words.

She was smaller than I thought she would be, but she was beautifully groomed. Her mane was black and trimmed short. And her grey coat was brushed perfectly.

"So you must be my servant boy," she said. And with a shake of her head, the donkey motioned for me to come closer.

It was a shock. To see her speak. And I think she knew how I was feeling.

"Why don't I tell you my story?" she suggested. "To put you at ease. And then you can fetch me a drink."

"All right," I nodded. It was exactly what I wanted to hear.

And she cleared her throat with a bray and a snort. "I was an ordinary donkey," she began. "The property of my master, Balaam. In those days, he was quite a popular figure. A mystical, magical man, who put curses on people for a fee."

"And they worked? These curses?" I asked.

"Amazingly, yes," she grinned. "But then you're

sitting here, talking to a donkey – so maybe you wouldn't find that so amazing after all.

"It was small stuff at first. Stopping cows from giving milk, chickens from laying eggs, sheep from giving birth. But as his reputation grew, so the jobs got bigger. And that's how we found ourselves on the way to a meeting with the kings of Midian and Moab."

"So you were with him from the start?" I asked.

"Oh yes," she nodded. "But it's not as if I had a choice. Not like today. I belonged to him. He had a whip. I carried him where he told me to go."

"And the kings?"

"The kings wanted him to put a curse on an entire nation," she continued. "The Israelites. We were off to seal the deal, but we ran into a little 'trouble' on the way."

"Bandits?" I asked. "Bad weather? Bad roads?"

"An angel," she whispered. And she smiled when she saw the look on my face.

"You're talking to a donkey," she reminded me. "How strange is an angel compared to that?" She had a point.

"So what did the angel do?"

"He tried to stop us," the donkey shrugged again. "He appeared out of nowhere in front of me, a drawn sword in his hand. And I did what any sensible donkey would do. I turned off the road and into a nearby field."

"And what did Balaam do?" I asked.

"He beat me with his whip." And I could see the hurt in her eyes.

"I have to admit, I was surprised," she continued. "Not by the beating. Balaam was not a patient man. No, what surprised me was his – how shall I put it? – ingratitude. I had just, as far as I could tell, saved his magical, mystical skin. And the whip was my reward."

"And you told him so?" I suggested.

"I said nothing at that moment. Not a hee. Not a haw. I simply turned back on to the road, by which time the angel had disappeared.

"I confess to having had a moment or two of doubt. Had the angel really been there? Had I perhaps been imagining things? It was a hot day, to be fair, and heat can do strange things to a donkey with a load on her back.

"Eventually, the road passed through a vineyard. There was a wall on one side and a wall on the other, with the road narrowing in between. And that's when the angel appeared again."

"So you couldn't turn off?"

"Precisely. The best I could do was to press up against one wall. And as I did so, I inadvertently crushed Balaam's foot against it."

She smiled. "It did seem like a just reward for the beating. But then he beat me again, and I decided that 'tit-for-tat' with a man and his whip was not the smartest game I could play.

"And – before you ask – no, I did not tell him off at that moment either.

"The road continued to narrow, the walls pressing in on both sides. And when we reached the point where there was no longer enough room to turn, the angel appeared for the third time.

"I had run out of options, to be honest. So I did what donkeys do when they reach that point: I dropped to my knees and refused to move any further."

"And Balaam…?"

"Oh, he beat me again. Beat me for all he was worth. Cursing and complaining and rueing the day he'd bought me.

"And, yes, that was the moment I opened my

mouth and spoke. 'What have I done?' I asked. 'To deserve three beatings?'"

"He must have been shocked," I said. "When he heard those words come from your mouth."

She grinned. "That's the interesting thing. He was so angry that I don't think he noticed at all. He just carried on ranting: 'You've made a fool of me! …

I'll miss my appointment! ... If I had a sword, I'd kill you!'

"So I ranted back, 'Am I not your donkey? ... Don't you trust me? ... Have I ever behaved this way before?'

"We were like some old married couple, arguing about our years together. I swear I heard the angel chuckle. But when he followed that by clearing his throat, everything changed.

"Balaam looked up and trembled and then bowed down. And it was clear that this was the first time he'd seen what was really going on."

"So the angel had been invisible to him?" I asked.

"It must have been," she answered. "An honest mistake on the part of the angel, I suppose. But it didn't take away the sting of those three beatings – a point that the angel proceeded to make on my behalf.

"Why did you beat your donkey?" he asked Balaam. "I came to stop you because you are travelling along a reckless path. Your donkey saw me and turned away. If she hadn't, I would certainly have killed you. Killed you and spared her."

"So did Balaam apologize to you?" I asked.

And she snorted – the biggest and longest snort so far.

"Not likely. No, he was too busy saving his magical, mystical skin. He apologized to the angel, of course.

And promised to go back home straightaway. But that's not what the angel wanted."

"No?" I asked, curious.

"No, the angel had obviously been sent by the God of the Israelites. And he had something he wanted Balaam to do.

"'Go and meet the kings,' the angel said. 'But only say what I tell you to.'"

"So you went to see the kings?"

"We went to see the kings. And that's when everything became clear. Every time they asked my

master to curse the people of Israel, he blessed them instead. It was funny. At least, I thought so. I tried to explain it all to the king's horses, but they just stood there and ignored me."

"Because you were talking like a human?" I asked.

"No," she brayed. "Because horses are stuck-up. I thought everybody knew that."

"Sorry," I apologized. "I didn't…"

"Not to worry," she hee-hawed. "Anything else you'd like to know?"

"Are you still in touch with Balaam?" I asked.

And she shook her head. "It was difficult after that. He had trouble getting work. As you can imagine, no one trusted him. My reputation, however, just kept on growing. You'd be amazed at how many people want to see a talking donkey."

"So Balaam set you free?"

And she threw back her head and laughed, a mouthful of teeth on show. "Set me free? I left! What did I need him for? A man with a whip? Puh-lease!

"And now I talk. People listen. If you must know, I'm the one who cracks the whip. Well, not literally – I couldn't hold one if I wanted to. But when I want something, all I have to do is stamp my hoof and it's there. I couldn't ask for more."

And then she laughed again. "Well, of course, I could ask – that's the point, isn't it? I'm a talking donkey."

"So do you ever hear from him then?"

And there was just the slightest hint of sadness in her eyes. "I didn't for a long while. And then, just last week, I received word that my former master is dead."

"No!"

"Yes. Seems as if he was desperate for work – any work. So he hooked up with the king of Moab again and was killed in battle – by the Israelites. Ironic, isn't it? All that angelic warning gone to waste.

"Didn't do me any harm, though, did it? And, on reflection, it does make me wonder: who was the real donkey after all?"

And with a stamp of her hoof, the story was over and the time for serving had begun.

"Now, how about that drink?" she brayed.

The Soldier's Version

The Battle of Jericho

"So how was work today?" I asked my dad. And he slammed his helmet on the table.

"Not good," he grunted. "Not good at all.

"I showed up on time at the walls of Jericho, ready for a day of killing and maiming. And then the priests arrived."

"Priests?" asked my mum. She was making dinner. Goat stew. "Why priests?"

"Some special secret plan," he sighed again. "That only Joshua, our commander, knows. It was like a parade. The priests went first. Then the guys on the ram's horn trumpets. Then the ark of the covenant."

"Ark of the covenant?" I said.

"Yeah, you know – the sacred box with the Ten Commandments inside," said my dad.

"So where were you?" asked my mum.

"Behind the ark," grumbled my dad.

"And the battering rams?" I asked excitedly. "Where were the battering rams?"

"Battering rams?" he scoffed. "There weren't any battering rams! I spoke to my mate Dave, who is second in command in the Battering Ram Division, and he told me that they'd been given the day off! Apparently, they had organized a picnic and they spent the day at a place of scenic beauty."

"Sounds lovely," nodded my mum.

"Not if you're trying to knock down a wall!" my dad shouted.

"So did you knock it down?" I asked.

"No, we didn't. We marched around the city. Once. The priests blew their trumpets. And then we went home. A right waste of time."

"Never mind, dear," said my

mum, spooning out the stew. "Eat your dinner. I'm sure things will be better tomorrow."

As it happens, things weren't.

"I'm raring to go!" he announced the next morning. "Itching to skewer a resident of Jericho – or two."

But when he got home from work that night, he was even more frustrated. And he was still itching.

"Flippin' fleas!" he moaned, slapping himself around the shoulders. "I spent the day fighting these things off. And that's all I fought!"

"So no battle then?" asked my mum. She was making dinner. Goat stew.

"No," he grumbled. "We just marched around the walls again. More priests and trumpets – and the ark, of course."

"And battering rams?" I asked hopefully.

Dad rolled his eyes. "Field trip, apparently. A bit of bird-watching. Some flower-gathering. That's what my mate Dave told me."

"So nothing got crushed?" I said.

And he squeezed a flea between his fingers. "Nothing but these blinkin' insects. And what's worse, the people of Jericho were laughing at us! They think this is some kind of joke."

"Maybe it's a clever plan," I suggested. "So they let their guard down for when you finally attack."

"IF we attack," he groaned.

"Never mind, dear," said my mum. "Here's your stew. Perhaps things will be better tomorrow."

But the next day was even worse.

"Don't ask!" shouted my dad, storming into our tent.

So we didn't. But it didn't help.

"I was desperate to destroy something!" he shouted again. "All we did was march around the city. Priests! Trumpets! Ark! And before anyone says it, the Battering Ram Division went to see a show!"

"A show?" asked my mum. She was making dinner. Goat stew.

"At the other end of the camp," he grunted. "There's a man with a monkey. He juggles, apparently.

"What, the monkey?" I asked.

"No, the man. I don't know! And I don't care! I just wanted to kill something. Not march around after a bunch of... of... trumpet-toting tabernacle attendants."

"Now that's a bit harsh, dear," tutted my mum. "My friend Betty heard them the other day and she said they were very good. There's a short beardy one on the end who is sometimes out of tune, but she reckons that the rest make a really nice sound. She told me that some of the people of Jericho even clapped. I think that says it all."

"They clapped because they're still alive!" cried my

dad. "If we were doing our job, they'd be screaming for mercy."

"I think someone needs to calm down, dear," she suggested. "Have some stew. I'm sure they'll let you dismember someone tomorrow."

When my dad got home the next day, he was cursing and scraping his helmet with a stick.

"Can't get the cheese off," he muttered.

"Cheesed off again, are we dear?" called my mum. She was making dinner. Goat stew.

"No!" he shouted. "Well, yes. What I said was, 'I can't get the cheese off.'"

She looked up from the cooking pot. "And why would there be cheese on your helmet, dear?" she asked. 'Did you murder a bit of gorgonzola today?'

"I wish I'd murdered something!" And then he sighed. "The truth is, I was late reporting for duty this morning."

My mum gasped. My dad was a good soldier. He was never late.

"I just didn't see the point," he explained. "Marching around that blasted city again."

"Did you get into trouble?" I asked.

"No. My sergeant is just as fed up as I am. But there was trouble, trust me. And this stinking cheese is the proof!

"Up until now, I have never marched with the soldiers at the very back. But if you get there late, that's where you go. And I had no idea of the kind of abuse they were getting from the people of Jericho."

"What kind?" I asked.

"They throw things," said my dad. "Sticks and stones at first. Fair enough. But then they chucked their rubbish at us. Pigs' trotters. Chicken beaks. Dog bones. You name it."

"Cheese?" guessed my mum.

"Buckets of the stuff," grunted my dad. "And really smelly, too."

I shuddered. "That must have been horrible."

"Nowhere near as horrible as what we'll do to them when we get inside that wall," he promised.

"And the Battering Ram Division?" asked mum.

"Manicures," muttered my dad, scraping away at his helmet. "And would you look at that? I just broke a nail. Typical."

My mum pushed a bowl in his direction. "Stew, dear. In your own time."

"Humiliating." That's all my dad said when he walked into the tent the next day.

"Did you lose your battle, dear?"

asked my mum. She was cooking dinner. Goat stew.

"What battle?" he grumbled. "There was no battle! Just another little march around the city."

"Priests," said my mum.

"Trumpets," I added.

"You've got the idea," my dad nodded.

"And the Battering Ram Division?" I asked.

"Making models," he sighed. "Though, to be fair, they were models of battering rams."

"That sounds good," said my mum.

"No," replied my dad, "because we're not DOING anything. And the people of Jericho just aren't afraid of us at all. In fact, today they even called us chickens."

"I think that's rather sweet," said my mum. "I have always found chickens to be delightful creatures with their cheery little clucks and that jaunty strutting gait. Now, goats, on the other hand –"

"It's an insult!" shouted my dad, flapping his arms and jerking his head about.

"Well, when you do it that way," replied my mum, "I can see what you mean. That's not attractive at all."

"It's an insult because they are saying that we are cowards!" he shouted again.

"I don't follow," she went on. "Corner a chicken and you are in for the fight of your life. Why, my own mother was pursued around the yard on more than one occasion by a pack of poultry. It took her years to recover. In fact, she still –"

"I don't care!" cried my dad. "It's an insult!"

"Maybe it's a warning," I suggested. "Maybe what they're saying is that there are giant chickens inside the walls, ready to crush you when you break through."

"A very good theory," nodded my mum. "See, dear, we both think that you are taking this far too personally. The people of Jericho were obviously saying that you are fierce and brave and to be feared."

"And a little jaunty," I added.

Dad shook his head. "I don't know…"

"Why don't you have a lie-down?" she suggested. "The stew will still be here when you wake up."

"Maybe I should," he muttered, trudging off.

As soon as he'd left, I looked at my mum. "I don't think he's a chicken," I said.

"No," she replied with a wink. "Bravest man I know. But he does struggle a bit with self-esteem."

When my dad came home from work the next night, he had a fierce and determined look in his eye. "Tomorrow!" he announced. "Tomorrow I am going to get to the bottom of this. Tomorrow is going to be different!"

"And why is that, dear?" asked my mum. She was making dinner. Goat stew.

"Because tomorrow my mate Dave is going to ask his boss to talk to Joshua – and then we're going to find out who came up with this crazy plan in the first place!"

"Your mate Dave in the Battering Ram Division?" I asked.

"Who spent the day in the hot springs at the other end of the camp," he sighed.

"While you marched around the city?" added my mum.

"I have stopped caring," he replied. "But tomorrow everything will be different. Because tomorrow, at least I will know who's responsible. And then… and then… I don't know – maybe somehow I'll be able to change things. Take control. Do something other than march around walls and eat goat stew every day!"

I thought for a moment that my mum was going to cry. But she held back the tears and replied quietly, "It's a very big goat."

My dad opened the tent flap and had a look.

"I'm sorry, darling," he whispered. "You're right. And it appears that we still have three legs to go. My apologies."

And so it was that when my dad came home that seventh day, things were indeed different.

He was grinning from ear to ear. "You'll never guess," he began.

"Oh, I think I can, dear," my mum smiled.

"We won the battle of course," he went on. "Jericho is finally ours. But the plan…"

"Was it Dave's?" I asked.

And he laughed. "No, Dave and the Battering Ram Division were in the hills picking fruit."

I was confused. "Then how did you knock down the walls?"

"Didn't have to," he chuckled. "Because the plan wasn't Dave's. It wasn't any of the commanders'. And it wasn't even Joshua's."

"Then whose plan was it, dear?" asked my mum.

71

"God's," he answered. "That's what Dave's boss told him anyway. And God's plan was that we should march around the city for six days in a row, blowing our trumpets, etcetera. And then, on the seventh day, that we should march around seven times, blow one long trumpet note, and give a shout. And that if we did that, the walls would just fall down."

"Which they did?" I asked.

"Which they did!" he grinned. "And then of course there was all the fighting and mopping up to do."

"So God had it under control the whole time, dear," said my mum. "All that complaining for nothing then."

"Yes, well…" he muttered. "The point is that we won."

"And that things are different now," she added, dishing out the dinner.

"Really?" he said, looking hopefully into his bowl.

"You can't expect to win every battle," she winked. "Now eat your goat stew, dear."

And he did.

The Detective's Version

Gideon and the Statue of Baal

It was midnight. The moon was full, but there were still shadows in the mean streets of Ophrah.

It had been a happy town, once. But then the Midianites had invaded, killing livestock, burning crops, and spreading fear.

I was working late, and that's why I saw it – a lone dark figure, creeping past my window as if he had something to hide.

I leaped to my feet, dagger in hand, and rushed to the door. But when I opened it, he was gone. So I stumbled into bed. But I did not sleep well. Not at all.

The name's Spade, by the way. Shemuel Spade. My business? Solving other people's problems.

I woke early the next morning. Someone was banging on the door.

I stumbled across the room. But when I opened the door, the sun blinded me for a moment, and I struggled to see who was there. Shadows again. The dark shadows of Ophrah. So I reached once more for my dagger.

"Hiya Shemuel!" the shadow said. And I put the dagger away. It was Ham, my errand boy and sometime assistant.

"How ya doing, kid?" I replied. And he really was a kid. Nine, maybe ten. I don't know. But he had a way with mysteries.

"Did you hear what happened?" he asked. And I shook my head.

"Sorry, kid," I grunted. "Rough night."

"It was a rough night in Ophrah, too," he announced. "You know that statue of Baal in the middle of town?"

I nodded. Don't have much time for religion, but if I want to worship a god, it will be the god of my own people – the God of Israel. Not some Midianite idol like Baal.

"Well, you'll never guess what happened," Ham went on. "Somebody knocked it down! Then they used the pieces to build an altar, and they sacrificed a bull on it.

"The people in the town who worship Baal are hopping mad. And everybody else is afraid that when the Midianites find out, they'll come looking for revenge. The town elders are on their way here to see if you can figure out who did it."

I smiled. Just a little. The elders had faith in me. I liked that. And I smiled for another reason, too. That shadow – the one who'd crept past my door in the night – I bet he had something to do with this. I was already on the case.

The town elders told me pretty much the same thing that the boy had. None of them had a clue who the culprit was. So I said goodbye and made my way to the scene of the crime.

Ophrah can be a tough town, but there were plenty of tears when I got to the altar. Baal-worshippers. Frightened citizens. And old Joash, who owned the burned-up bull.

"What a mess," I grunted.

And Ham just nodded.

I interviewed anyone who would talk to me, but nobody had seen anything. "The middle of the night." That's all anyone said. And I couldn't get the picture of that mysterious stranger out of my head.

The boy tapped me on the back. "Have you seen this?" he asked. And he pointed to the ground.

Sure enough, there was a footprint – a single,

purple footprint − on a stone slab.

"What do you think it means?" he asked.

And I shook my head. "Don't know. Might belong to the perpetrator. But why is it purple? And why is there only one?"

Visions of a hideous, hopping, purple-footed fiend filled my mind. And I wracked my brains to remember – had that mysterious stranger moved on two feet or one?

"Maybe he just put one foot on the slab," suggested Ham. "And the next one landed in the dirt."

It was an explanation that had some merit. It was sorely lacking in drama, though.

"No, we're looking for a one-footed man," I said. "Or someone who goes about on one foot. A hopper."

"But I don't think there's anybody like that in town," the boy replied. "And why would he leave a purple stain behind?"

The boy was eager, but lacking in experience.

"Obviously he came from another town," I explained. "That's why we've never seen him before. As for the purple stain, I think that maybe he comes from a town where they paint themselves purple. A purple hopping person from a purple hopping town. Where they hate Baals and bulls and Midianites. Find that town and we find our man."

I grinned. That was my first guess. And my first guesses were almost always right.

Ham scratched his head. "But I've never heard of a purple hopping town. Couldn't it be something simpler? Couldn't he have just – I don't know – stepped in something purple?"

I patted the boy on the head with an understanding smile. I'd been young once. And innocent. How could I explain to him that the world was a complicated place?

"You go and look for your purple puddle," I humoured him. "And I'll ask around about that hopping town. See you later, kid." And we went our separate ways.

He caught up with me a couple of hours later.

"I think I've found something!" he said excitedly.

"Calm down, kid," I replied. "Let's have it, one step at a time."

"I remembered what you said about the puddle," he began. And I couldn't help but chuckle. The kid didn't even get the joke.

"So I asked myself," he went on, "where I could find a purple puddle? And it came to me right away. In a wine press! That's where people squish the juice out of grapes, yeah? So I went to the wine press."

I shook my head. "Sorry to disappoint you, kid, but there must be dozens of people who have used that wine press. There's no way we can narrow it down to one. And besides, I just talked with someone who has a cousin who lives in a bouncing town. And where there are bouncers, there must be hoppers…"

But the kid ignored me. He wouldn't let go of the wine press thing.

"I thought of that," he continued. "But for the print to be left behind, the person's foot would have had to have been wet. Which means he would have been in the wine press the same day the statue got wrecked."

"That's a fair assumption," I nodded.

"And the only person anybody could remember seeing near the wine press that day," he concluded, "was Gideon, the son of Joash."

It was all I could do not to laugh.

"Hang on, kid," I said. "Two problems here. One, the burned-up bull belonged to Gideon's father. Two, Gideon is just about the biggest coward this town has ever seen. He wouldn't say 'boo' to a goose. He wouldn't get close enough to a goose so the goose would hear him say 'boo'. He'd hide somewhere the goose would never find him and not even bother saying 'boo' in the first place."

"Somewhere like a wine press maybe?" the boy asked.

"We're not talking about geese

79

here!" I reminded him. "We're talking about tearing down a foreign idol and setting fire to livestock and making people really angry! People who will then show up at your door and do painful things to you. Gideon is the last person who would dare to do that."

"Maybe so," said Ham. "But he might be the first person to hide in a wine press! I don't see how it could hurt to talk to him."

The kid was stubborn. I liked that. Reminded me a bit of me. But I didn't think it would do him any harm to see how wrong-headed his little theory was. So I nodded my head and off we went.

When we arrived at Gideon's house, the kid got all excited again.

"Look! Look!" he shouted, pointing to another rocky slab. "A purple footprint, just like the first one! And did you see this? Bits of grain or something stuck to it."

"Calm down," I cautioned him. "It might be a coincidence. Or maybe that purple hopping town has sent a load of spies our way."

"But I can prove it's the same," he insisted. And he held up a broken stick.

"I used this to measure the first footprint," he explained. Then he laid it beside the new print and started shouting again. "It matches! It's the same length! Look!"

I was about to suggest the possibility of purple

hopping twins when the door flew open and old Joash started shouting as well. "What's going on here? What do you want? Have you found that bull-burner yet?"

I shook my head. "No, but the boy here has this crazy notion that it was your son, Gideon. Claims he can match the footprint on your doorstep to the one at the scene of the crime."

And that's when the blubbering started. "I'm sorry, Father! I should have told you. I can explain, honest."

It was Gideon, weeping like a baby.

I looked at Ham and he just smiled.

"Beginner's luck," I thought. But I didn't say it. I just smiled back with a "Well done, kid."

And then it all came out. Seems that Gideon had been hiding in the wine press, threshing wheat in one corner, so the Midianites couldn't steal it. An angel appeared to him (I've heard stranger alibis) and told him that the God of Israel had chosen him to defeat the Midianites. And that, as his first act, he was to tear down the statue of Baal and sacrifice a bull to the God of Israel on the ruins.

It was the craziest story I'd ever heard. God choosing the biggest coward in town to defeat a whole army of invaders. Really? But his father bought it. And so did everybody else in Ophrah.

They wanted to kill him at first, but then his father said, "If Baal was a real god, why didn't he stop Gideon from tearing down the statue?"

Fair point, that. And they let Gideon go. Even gave him a nickname – Jerubbaal – which means something like "let Baal save himself".

Case closed then? Not quite. Gideon claimed he never walked past my house that night, and I never did discover who the mysterious moonlight stranger was.

So I went home and locked my door. Then, with my dagger at my side, I fell into an uneasy sleep.

And dreamed. Of the mean streets of Ophrah. And hoppers…

The Official Version

David and Goliath

When my mum told me that I was going to be apprenticed to her brother in the Israelite army, I thought that I would learn how to be a soldier.

I could not have been more wrong.

"There are two ways to get ahead in this man's army," he told me the very first morning. "Kill as many of the enemy as possible. Or work your bottom off to make things run more efficiently."

I looked at my uncle. He couldn't have weighed more than fifty kilos. And he wasn't even carrying a sword. It didn't take a genius to figure out that his job had to do with option number two. And so, now, did mine.

He handed me a soft clay tablet and a stylus. "You might want to take notes." he suggested.

"I am responsible for two areas, as far as the army of Israel is concerned," he began. "The first has to do with the general well-being of the soldiers. Keeping them fit and making sure that there is as little illness as possible."

"Health, then," I wrote on my tablet.

"My job is also to protect them from any unnecessary accidents," he went on. "You may think a battlefield is dangerous. But you would be surprised at the number of injuries that are sustained behind the lines. Tripping over misplaced shields. Falling onto badly positioned spears. I've seen it all. And it is my job to keep such incidents to a minimum."

"Safety, then," I wrote on my tablet. "Health. And Safety."

"I couldn't have put it better myself," my uncle grinned. "You learn quickly, boy. A bit like me, even if I say so myself. You'll have no trouble getting ahead."

Then he took me on his morning inspection.

"Who does this helmet belong to?" he asked. "It needs to be picked up and put in its place. Helmet accidents account for 15 per cent of injuries in the average battalion. And this sandal? Who left this sandal here? Someone could trip and fall."

He went on like this for an hour – shouting out violations and listing them on his own tablet as he went. The strange thing was that none of the soldiers seemed to pay him any attention.

"Yes, I know," he said when I asked. "It's quite normal for them to swear and spit on the ground when I point out their errors. No one likes to be criticized. And, speaking of criticism," he added, interrupting himself, "what is that boy doing here?"

There was, indeed, a boy. About ten years old, maybe eleven. And he was carrying bread and cheese.

"You there!" my uncle shouted. "Who are you and what are you doing here?"

"His name's David," grunted a soldier nearby. "He's a shepherd. And he's also my brother."

"And mine," grunted the soldier next to him.

"And mine, too," a third soldier chimed in.

"You're all his brothers?" my uncle asked.

And three heads nodded in unison.

"Well, he's too young to serve in the army," said my uncle. "And his presence here is a potential danger to you, as well as to himself. This is no place for a child!"

"But he's brought our lunch," the first brother replied.

"Ah, yes, lunch," noted my uncle, eyeballing the

bread and cheese. Then he scribbled something on his tablet and continued.

"So where was this cheese produced? And what about the bread? Were work surfaces clean? Was the milk fresh? Was the flour free of bacteria?"

The soldier brothers looked at one another, confused.

"Dunno," one of them answered. "It came from our family's farm, I think."

"Ah, the family farm, " my uncle sighed, scribbling on his tablet again. "The most common source of disease in this man's army. No inspections. No certificates. Just good old mum and dad and their unwashed hands and germ-filled bowls and spoons."

Then he turned to the boy and reached for the cheese. "I'm afraid I'm going to have to take that," he said.

At once, three enormous soldier-brothers moved around us, in a circle.

"It's our lunch," the first brother repeated. And he said it as if he meant it. As if he might just eat us instead.

"Yes, well…" my uncle replied, sizing up the situation. "Perhaps I can let you off with a warning just this once. But you will be required to attend a course on soldierly hygiene. I'll expect you all at my tent next Monday. Ten o'clock sharp!"

The circle opened. We retreated. But my uncle didn't act as if it had been a retreat at all.

"A bit of give and take," he whispered to me as we hurried away. "That's what you need if you want to get ahead in this man's army."

"But it seems as if we did all the giving and they did all the taking," I replied.

"It may look that way," he grinned. "But we have sown a seed, challenged the way they think. And that hygiene course? It lasts for hours. With no breaks!"

Just then, the boy rushed past us.

"Where is he going now?" my uncle demanded to know.

"Off to see the king!" said one of the three brothers, rushing after him. "To ask if he can fight the giant!"

"Giant?" asked my uncle. "What giant?"

"That giant!" replied a soldier on the line, pointing across the battlefield.

We looked. There was, indeed, a giant standing there.

"His name's Goliath," the soldier explained. "He is the most powerful and most feared warrior in the Philistine army. He has challenged us to send a champion of our own to fight him. If he wins, we all become his slaves. I thought everybody knew that."

"Some of us are concerned with a more important battle," my uncle proudly proclaimed. "The battle against food poisoning and the odd accidental fall." Then he snapped his fingers. "And if that shepherd boy reaches the king," he said, "there is no telling what damage he might do. Shepherds are not known for their cleanliness. Ticks. Fleas. Who knows what tiny pests that boy is carrying? And if they should hop off onto the king? Well... I think we need to make haste."

So we rushed after the shepherd and his brother, but by the time we reached the king's tent, they had already gone inside.

My uncle was determined, though. He pushed past the king's guards, waving his tablet in their faces and shouting, "Official business! Make way! Must get through!"

And when we burst into the tent, there was the shepherd boy – wearing the king's armour!

"Your Majesty!" cried my uncle. "I must insist that you stop this at once. Fleas! Ticks...!"

"Calm down, soldier," the king commanded. "The boy wants to fight the giant. I'm just giving him a fighting chance."

"But he's not even old enough to serve in the army!" my uncle pleaded.

"He says he's killed a lion and a bear," replied the king. "That takes some doing."

"Begging your pardon, sir," my uncle countered, "we have only his word for this. Now, if he were wearing a bearskin or sporting a lion's pelt…"

"We would definitely have to check for fleas," I whispered.

"Well done, boy," my uncle whispered back. "You're getting the hang of this. You'll most certainly get ahead."

And then the boy dropped the armour on the floor. "Don't need this," he shrugged. "The Lord God helped me defeat the lion and the bear. He'll help me beat the giant, too." Then he pulled a sling out of his belt. "This is all I need. This and a few good stones." And, with that, he marched out of the tent.

"Your Majesty!" my uncle cried again. "That is an unauthorized weapon! It hasn't been tested and certified. You can't let him use that!"

"The boy's got guts," the king nodded. "I'll give him that. And if he wants to face that giant with a sling and a few stones, well… may the Lord God be with him. All I know is that I want to see how this goes." And he marched out of the tent as well.

"Your Majesty," my uncle went on, following behind. "The slingshot may be an appropriate device for farm and field, where the only victim of a badly aimed projectile would be an unfortunate sheep or goat. But a field of battle, crammed with soldiers and their support staff, is no place for such a tool. In short, Your Majesty, HE COULD PUT SOMEBODY'S EYE OUT!"

"Let's hope it's the giant's, then," the king laughed, as we moved to the edge of the battlefield.

The shepherd boy ran toward the giant, and the giant laughed as well. But it was not a nice laugh.

"Do you mock me?" he roared at the Israelites. "Do you think I am a dog? Is that why you send this stick of a boy to fight me? Come closer, lad, and I will feed your flesh to the birds."

"This does not look good," I whispered.

"No," my uncle nodded. "Feeding meat to creatures that are accustomed to eating grain is likely to result in serious health issues."

The boy was not worried, though.

"I come against you in the name of the Lord God of Israel!" he cried. And, placing a stone in his sling, he swung it around his head and let it fly.

"Duck, Your Majesty!" cried my uncle. "The stone could easily come this way."

But it didn't. It hurtled through the air and struck

the giant right between the eyes. He fell to the ground at once, and when he did, the shepherd boy ran to his side, grabbed his sword, and cut off his head!

Everyone cheered. The king included. Everyone but my uncle, who tut-tutted and ticked off rows of boxes on his tablet.

"I count seventeen separate violations of our health and safety codes," he sighed. "It's a miracle that no one was hurt."

"Well, there was the giant," I noted.

And he ticked off another box. "Make that eighteen violations," he added.

And that's when the shepherd boy returned, dragging the giant's head.

"What shall I do with this?" he asked the king.

And the king pointed to my uncle. "Give it to him. He'll know how to dispose of it. Safely, yes?" he chuckled.

"Of course, Your Majesty," my uncle said, bowing. "I would consider it an honour to serve you in this manner."

"See," he winked at me. "I told you this job was the way to get ahead!"

The Widow's Version

Elijah and the Widow

Ever since my dad died, I've sort of had to look out for my mum.

There's the famine, of course. We've been hungry for months, now. More than hungry, actually. Starving.

No sign of rain. Not a cloud in the sky. And no rain means no crops. And no food.

But that's not the only problem with mum.

I mean, I love her. She's amazing. She's kind and caring and everything you'd want your mum to be. But, as my gran says, she is sometimes lacking a bit

SNIFF SNIFF

in the common-sense department. Especially where men are concerned.

I get it. She needs a man about the house to do the odd job. A handyman. But why does she have to hire so many losers?

There was that guy from Tyre, for example, whose hobby was collecting and preserving strangely shaped sheep droppings. Or whatshisname from Sidon, who would only eat fish that started with the letter A. Or that man from Gath

who insisted that he was the great-great-great-grandson of the giant Goliath. Yeah, right. He was hardly taller than me! Fortunately, they all turned out to be pretty useless – so they didn't last long.

You can imagine my dismay, however, when she came home last week and announced that she'd met yet another man whose help, she was sure, would be indispensable.

I sighed. "Where'd you meet him, Mum?"

"By the city gates," she answered merrily.

"Not from around here then?" I asked.

"No. Don't think so," she smiled. "He's an Israelite."

Do you see what I mean? No common sense.

"Mum," I said as firmly as I thought I should. "Mum, we live in Zarephath. We're Phoenicians. Israelites don't actually like us very much. And particularly not our religion."

She looked up, as if she was thinking about my answer. As if she was looking for a reply. And she was still smiling.

"But didn't our lovely Princess Jezebel marry Ahab, the Israelite king?"

"Yes, she did," I nodded. "But that was just politics, Mum. To make a bit of peace. We're still not what you would call 'fond' of Israelites."

"I don't see why not?" she chirped. "Elijah is a sweet man – you'll see."

"So his name is Elijah?" I asked. "And his job…?"

"He's a prophet," she replied.

"A prophet?" I repeated.

"Yes, he speaks for God," she smiled.

"The Israelite God?" I queried. "The one who specializes in smiting the Israelites' enemies?"

"That would be the one," she nodded. "And, according to Elijah, he is also the one who is responsible for the drought."

I sat down. This was going to be a long conversation.

"The drought we are currently suffering?" I asked, just a little agitated. "The drought that led to the famine? The famine that led to our present starving situation? The starving situation that will shortly lead to our deaths?"

And again she nodded. "Yes."

"This is the man you have invited to help out around the house?" I cried.

"Yes. Actually, I've invited him to supper tonight," she mumbled. "Well, to share our bread."

"WE HAVE NO BREAD!" I shouted. "Because there is a famine. Because there is a drought. Because the God of your new friend Elijah apparently stopped the rain from falling!"

She shrugged. "Well, when you put it that way, it doesn't sound so nice. But that is still no reason not to give him a chance. After all, he's hungry, too."

"Good," I grunted. "Serves him right."

"I'm not so sure," she went on. "I mean, as long as the ravens were feeding him, he was fine…"

"Ravens?" I interrupted. "He was fed by ravens?"

"On the far side of the Jordan River," she nodded. "Yes. He says they would bring him bread and meat in the morning, and then more bread and meat at night."

"Mum," I sighed. "Are you sure this guy is a prophet? C'mon. Man Sustained by Sandwich-bearing Birds? He sounds like a nutter to me. Or a liar. Or both."

She patted me on the shoulder.

(I hate it when she does that.) And then she said, "I don't care if he's a liar. Or a nutter. Or a prophet. Or even where he comes from. We need the help. He only wants a bit of bread. And I think we should give him some."

My mum. Men. There was no talking to her. I don't even know why I tried.

"All right," I agreed. "Let's scrape together what we've got and make some bread."

So I grabbed the jar of flour. She grabbed the jug of oil. And as she did, she snapped her fingers and smiled again.

"I know you're not going to believe this," she said. "But the prophet told me something else."

I shook my head. "Let me guess. He has a third eye on his elbow? He was raised by whales? He rides about in a chariot made of fire?"

"Nothing as silly as that!" she grinned. "No, when I explained to him that we didn't have much food left, he told me that the God of Israel would make sure that our jar of flour and jug of oil would not run out until the rains began to fall again."

"Still pretty silly," I replied. "Will ravens be filling them then?"

"Let's just make the bread," she said.

So we did. And I know you are going to find this as hard to believe as I did – but I could never get that jar to empty. Or the jug either.

We made Elijah a loaf. And one for ourselves as well. And when we had finished, somehow there was more flour and oil than when we had started!

"Well, Mum," I said. "I've got to hand it to you. He didn't sound promising at first, but I think there might be a future for us and this Elijah fellow."

My mum picked up a piece of camel-shaped sheep poo. "I know you haven't always approved of my choice of handymen," she winked. "But I think I've done all right this time. How about we ask him to stay with us for a while? We could use the help. And, like I always say, it never hurts to have a prophet about the place."

"You've never said that," I sighed.

"Well, I'm saying it now," she replied. And she opened the door and called, "Elijah! Coo-eee! Bread's ready! Come and get it!"

What can I say? I don't always understand her, but I love my mum.

Grandad's Version

Elijah and the Prophets of Baal

My grandad leaned back against the wall and looked at the ceiling.

"I suppose I've always been a fan of the underdog," he mused.

I could feel a story coming. I searched in vain for a way out. But Mum was making dinner and I had a pile of vegetables to chop. So I was stuck.

"When I was your age, young Malachi, I was sport mad. But it was always the underdog I supported. And I have no regrets."

"So what football team was it, then?" I asked.

It seemed the polite thing to do. And the pile of veggies was huge.

"Football?" he snorted. "Football! Why, we didn't have those fancy shmancy footballs in my day, boy. Balls made of skin – stuffed and sewn together? You don't know how lucky you are."

"So what did you kick?" I asked.

"Coneys, boy! Rock badgers! We'd catch one of those critters, set him in the middle of the pitch, and see who could kick him to the other side."

"Sounds cruel to me," said my mum.

"And so it was!" replied Grandad. "Those little beasties could bite! You'd put your boot in – but of course we didn't have boots in those days, just our bare feet – and the coney would clamp his teeth around your big toe. I can't begin to describe the pain."

"Well, maybe if you hadn't been trying to kick them…" I suggested.

"My point exactly, boy. The underdog! Or rather the under-coney. That's whose side I was on. So one day, when my mates were chasing one of the little critters, I swooped in, scooped him up off the ground, and just started running with him. And when I stumbled into the goal, everyone cheered and picked me up and hoisted me onto their shoulders."

"Because you saved the coney?" asked my mum.

"No! Because I'd inadvertently invented a new way of playing the game. My mates were fed up with having their toes gnawed, so they changed the rules. And from that point on, you could either Kick the Coney or Carry the Coney."

"But didn't the coneys just bite your thumbs instead of your toes?" I asked.

"You're getting ahead of me, boy," he scowled. "Never get ahead of an old man and his story."

"Sorry," I muttered.

"And yes," he continued. "They did bite our thumbs – and that resulted in my final innovation, Tossing the Coney. It was a natural reaction at first. They'd chomp on your thumb – you'd chuck them in the air. But before long, coneys were flying all over the field – as a proper part of the game."

"And they liked that better than being kicked or carried?" asked my mum.

"The flying, yes," Grandad smiled. "You could see the expressions of delight and joy on their little coney faces."

Then he shook his head. "But the landing, not so much."

"Well, I'm glad we just kick balls today," I said.

"And that we have water," added Grandad.

"Water?" said my mum.

"That's right. In my day there was a drought so

bad that it didn't rain for three whole years. Dirt. That's all we had. Dirt plates and dirt spoons and dirt houses and dirt sandwiches – or maybe they were made of sand, I forget.

It was something we scraped off the ground."

"When was that, Grandad?"

"The Days of Elijah,"

he nodded. "Those were the days. Of Elijah."

"He was a prophet, wasn't he?" said my mum.

"One of the best prophets Israel ever had," Grandad replied. "In fact, they say that he was the one who stopped the rain. Well, God did it, I suppose – but it was Elijah that told evil King Ahab and even evil-er Queen Jezebel that it was going to happen."

"Why were they evil?" I asked.

"Because they got our people to stop worshipping the true God and to worship Baal instead."

"Baal?" I said.

"That's right, Baal," Grandad nodded. "It rhymes with 'pail'. Although some folks insist that it's actually Baal, which rhymes with… well… 'ball'. It's confusing really – but all you need to know is that he was some foreign fertility god."

"Fertility?" I asked. And Grandad blushed.

"Erm… you'll have to ask your mum about that," he muttered.

Mum looked at Grandad and shook her head. Then said, matter-of-factly, "They believed he made the crops grow."

I scratched my head. "But I thought the true God of Israel did that."

"And so he does, boy," Grandad grinned. "But in those days – the Days of Elijah – there weren't many of us who believed that. So Elijah arranged a little competition, between himself and the prophets of Baal, to prove whose god was more powerful. And I'm sure you can guess whose side I was rooting for."

"The coneys'?" I answered.

"No! The underdog's! Elijah – that's who I supported. Don't know where this fixation with coneys came from."

"But you…"

"Don't interrupt an old man in the middle of his story, boy. Now where was I? Oh, yeah – four hundred and fifty. That's how many prophets of Baal there were. And only one Elijah.

"The competition was held at the top of Mount Carmel. Each side had a bull and a pile of wood. The bulls were killed and chopped up into pieces and placed on the wood…"

"More animal cruelty," sighed my mum.

"And then each side was given the chance to call on their god to send fire down from heaven and burn up the bulls!"

"That sounds amazing!" I gasped. "Were you there?"

"Everybody was there!" Grandad beamed. "But most of the people, my mates included, were supporting the Baals.

"They had big Bs painted on their chests and waved bright Baal banners and even chanted their noisy Baal songs.

"I can remember it like it was yesterday. 'Baal, Baal, he can't fail!'

"Or in the case of those who preferred the alternative pronunciation, 'Baal, Baal, he can't fall!'

"Honestly, if you're going to worship a deity, you ought to be able to agree on how to say his name."

"But what did your mates do when they found out that you supported the God of Israel?" I asked.

"What do you think?" he sighed. "They called me names. They laughed at me. They threw things at me. Things made of dirt, mostly."

"And coneys?" I suggested.

Grandad scowled. "You're making me sorry I brought that up, boy. But, yes, there was the odd airborne coney. So I just stood off by myself, waving my little 'Go Jehovah!' flag. And then I caught Elijah's eye."

"Did he wave to you or anything?" I asked.

"More than that," Grandad grinned. "He came over to me. He thanked me for my support. He told me that there were hundreds just like me who supported him too. And that if we walked through the storm, and kept our chins up high, and weren't afraid of the dark, and held hope in our hearts, that we would never walk alone."

"You'll never walk alone." said my mum, brushing a tear from her eye. "That's very moving."

"So what happened?" I said. "Who won?"

"You're getting ahead of me again, boy," Grandad muttered. "This is a story worth telling one step at a time.

"The prophets of Baal went first…"

"They must have won the coney toss," I chuckled.

"The prophets of Baal went first," he repeated, ignoring my remark. "And they prayed to their god all morning, dancing around the bull. But nothing happened. Not a thing. So Elijah started to taunt them. You know, make fun of them.

" 'Maybe you need to shout louder,' he suggested. 'Maybe Baal's deep in thought. Maybe he's busy. Maybe he's on holiday. Maybe he's gone for a wee.' "

"I bet that made your mates angry," I said.

"My mates? Yeah, they were angry all right. But that was nothing compared to the prophets of Baal. They grabbed their swords and spears and started cutting themselves. They shouted louder and louder. There was noise and there was blood and…"

"I think that's enough, Dad," suggested my mum. "We get the idea."

112

"All right then," he sighed. "I was just painting a picture for the boy. It's not like we saw intestines or anything…"

"Dad!"

"Or spleens," he muttered. "All right, it was messy. We'll leave it at that. The point is that nothing happened. Baal didn't answer. So Elijah told everyone to come to him. He took twelve stones, one for each of the tribes of Israel, and repaired an old altar to God that had been broken down. He put the wood and the bull pieces on the altar. And then he dug a trench around the altar."

"A trench?" I said. "What for?"

Grandad chuckled. "You won't believe it. My mates didn't, that's for sure. He told someone to fill four big jars with water and dump them on the bull and on the wood."

"The wood that was supposed to catch fire?" I asked.

"That's right," Grandad nodded.

"And all that water – in a drought?" added my mum. "What a waste."

Grandad nodded again. "And what a risk. You could hear the people moaning."

"So what did Elijah do?" I asked.

"The same thing again," Grandad answered. "More jugs. More water. And then he did it a THIRD time! And there was so much water on the altar that it ran down and filled up the trench.

"Now it was my mates who were laughing. There was no way that mess was going to catch fire. And they knew it.

"But Elijah didn't seem bothered at all. He stepped forward, he looked to heaven, and he prayed:

" 'Lord of Abraham, Isaac, and Jacob, show these people that you are the true God. Answer my prayer so that they will turn back to you.' "

"And then?" I said. "Then what happened?"

"Then he winked at me, boy. Me and my little 'Go Jehovah!' flag. And before I could wave back or anything, fire fell from heaven. Fire so hot and so fierce that it burned up the bull and the wood and the stones and the soil and every bit of water in that trench!"

"Wow! And what did your friends do?"

"They fell on their faces, with everybody else on that mountain, and cried, 'The Lord – he is God! The Lord – he is God!' Well, everybody but the four hundred and fifty prophets of Baal. They thought it might be a good time to exit the pitch."

"So they got away?"

"Nah. The people hunted them down and killed them all."

"A bit extreme," noted my mum.

"It was a different era," Grandad shrugged.

"Relegation hadn't been invented yet."

"Well, thanks for the story," said my mum. "And you can stay for dinner, if you like."

"Much appreciated," Grandad replied, "but I need to stretch my legs." Then he turned to me.

"I wouldn't mind a bit of that turnip you've been chopping up, though."

"Sure," I said. And I tossed him a piece. "But it's not cooked."

"Oh, it's not for me," he chuckled. And he reached into his pocket and pulled out… a coney!

"Who's been a good boy, then?" he coo-ed, stroking the coney under its chin. "And here's a little treat for you."

Then Grandad stood up, the coney nibbled on the turnip, and they walked out of the house.

And the last thing I heard was, "Owww! That's not a turnip, that's my thumb! I think somebody needs to do a little flying. Wheeeeee…!"

Nigel's Version

The Young Men at the Court of Babylon

The five friends sat nervously together in the hall of the palace.

"What are we doing here?" asked Daniel.

"We're supposed to be slaves, right?" said Hananiah.

"That's what I thought," whispered Mishael. "The Babylonians destroyed Jerusalem and dragged us here to Babylon."

"So why are we in a palace?" wondered Azariah.

And Saul just grunted, "I'm hungry."

Just then a very important-looking man strolled into the room.

"My name is Ashpenaz," he announced. "And I will be in charge of your training."

"Training?" asked Daniel.

And before anyone else could speak, Ashpenaz answered, "That's right, my boy. Training. Or, to be more specific, the very best education that Babylon has to offer."

"But why?" asked Hananiah. "When you destroyed our country and carried our people off as slaves?"

Ashpenaz chuckled. And when he did, his big belly jiggled. And his jowly face as well.

"My dear boy," he began. "We Babylonians are not monsters. You have nothing to fear from us. We are a powerful people, and the destruction of your country is proof of that. But we want you to be happy here. You and all the other Judeans we have brought to work in our fair land. In fact, we want you to become good Babylonians yourselves. You will, after all, be here for a very long time.

"So we will teach you – you, the sons of the finest families from your land – what it means to be Babylonians. And it is our hope that you will come to call our home your home, too. And that all your people here will follow your lead."

"So you want us to forget our country?" asked Mishael.

"And our traditions?" added Azariah.

"It's the only way," smiled Ashpenaz. But it wasn't the friendliest of smiles.

"Is there anything for lunch?" asked Saul.

And now Ashpenaz beamed. "All in good time, my boy. But first, I'd like you to read this." And he handed each boy a little scroll.

"Back in a jiff," he concluded, beaming again at Saul. "And then we'll have a bite to eat."

Daniel read his scroll. "They're giving me a new name," he said. "A Babylonian name. From now on, I'm called Belteshazzar."

"I'm called Shadrach," said Hananiah.

"I'm Meshach," said Mishael.

"Abednego," said Azariah. "And what are they calling you, Saul?" he asked.

And Saul just shrugged and grunted, "I can't quite make it out, but it looks like Nigel."

At that moment, Ashpenaz stuck his head out of a nearby doorway and called, "Dinner's ready, boys. Eat it while it's hot!"

And Belteshazzar, Shadrach, Meshach, Abednego, and Nigel trooped into the dining room.

There were boys from every nation gathered there – from each country that the Babylonians had conquered. And right in the middle stood an empty table, set with five places.

The boys sat down and just stared at the food. It looked amazing. And smelled even better.

"Enjoy!" grinned Ashpenaz. Then he set about chatting with the other boys.

Nigel rubbed his hands together. "About time. And just look at that meat! Let's dig in."

But the others just sat there, motionless.

"You know we can't eat that meat," whispered Belteshazzar.

"I know," Shadrach whispered back. "It's been dedicated to the Babylonian gods."

"And if we eat it," added Meshach, "it's like saying that they're our gods, too."

"And there is only one God," Abednego concluded, "the God of our people, the Maker of heaven and earth."

Meshach

Abednego

Nigel

"C'mon!" cried Nigel. "Enough of the religious stuff! The gravy's getting cold!"

But Belteshazzar had already marched over to Ashpenaz. "I'm sorry," he announced. "But we cannot eat the food you have served us."

"What? Not rich enough for you?" Ashpenaz said in surprise.

"No, it looks amazing," said Belteshazzar. "But there is a problem…" And he explained everything to Ashpenaz.

"I understand your difficulty," Ashpenaz replied. "But if you are going to learn to be good Babylonians, then you will have to eat what Babylonians eat."

"I see," Belteshazzar nodded. And he returned to the table.

"He says we have to eat it," Belteshazzar sighed.

"But we can't," said Shadrach.

"There has to be another way," said Meshach.

"Either that or we starve," added Abednego. "What do you think, Nigel?"

"Mmphhh-mmph," mumbled Nigel, his mouth full of something.

Belteshazzar snapped his fingers. "I've got it!" he announced. "We have a contest. We eat simple food – water and vegetables – stuff that they don't dedicate to their gods. And we show them that we can be even more healthy by doing that!"

"So we teach them something," added Shadrach.

"And we still honour our God!" said Meshach.

"Perfect!" Abednego concluded.

"Are you guys crazy?" Nigel belched. "This grub is incredible! Wake up and smell the sausages!"

Belteshazzar called Ashpenaz over to the table and explained the contest to him. And when he did, every hint of a smile disappeared from Ashpenaz's face.

"This is very unusual," he said. "The king has commanded me to take care of you. If this contest makes you ill, he will have my head."

"Trust us," said Belteshazzar. "At the end of ten days, we will be healthier than any of these other boys."

"And hungrier," mumbled Nigel.

"What was that?" said Abednego.

"Just my tummy grumbling," Nigel replied.

"So you are all agreed on this course of action?" asked Ashpenaz, looking especially hard at Nigel.

"We are!" said Shadrach.

"Then so be it," Ashpenaz agreed. And he ordered the servants to remove everything but vegetables from the table.

"There goes the duck," Nigel sighed. "And the plum sauce. And the roast beef. And the lovely, lovely gravy."

On the first day, all the other boys had…

"Venison," drooled Nigel. "Venison in a wine and pomegranate reduction."

"Eat your broccoli," said Belteshazzar. "It's good for you."

On the second day, all the other boys had…

"Partridge," drooled Nigel. "I don't suppose I could just have one forkful, could I?"

"Not when this turnip stew is so delicious!" chirped Shadrach.

On the third day, all the other boys had…

"Steak!" drooled Nigel. "Thick, fat, juicy steak! Haven't any of you ever heard the saying 'When in Babylon, do what the Babylonians do'?"

"That's a new one to me," mumbled Meshach through a mouthful of sprouts.

And so it continued on the fifth (Camel Chops vs Cabbage), sixth (Fried Chicken vs Beetroot), seventh (Curried Lamb vs Leek), and eighth (Hunter's Pie vs Lettuce) days… so that by the ninth day, Nigel could hardly control himself.

"I don't care!" he cried, as all the other boys dug into their roast beef. "Surely it's important to

respect the way that other people live, and to learn to appreciate what's good about it. It's all about tasting… yes, tasting – that's the perfect word – tasting those differences for ourselves! We shouldn't be bound by what our parents or our religions say, but free to decide for ourselves."

"An open-minded viewpoint," grinned Ashpenaz, who happened to be wandering by. "Very admirable, my boy," he added, dangling a juicy bit of beef in front of Nigel's face.

"Don't do it!" pleaded Belteshazzar. "They want us to forget everything that's important to us – our home, our history, our God!"

"Nonsense," grinned Ashpenaz. "We just want you to be exactly like us." Then he dipped the beef into the gravy boat. And that's when Nigel snapped.

He grabbed the beef and the gravy, dashed off to one of the other tables, and stuffed himself until he could hardly breathe.

"Day ten tomorrow," sneered Ashpenaz. "Then we'll see who is happy and who is healthy, and who is not."

When the morning came, Ashpenaz called the five friends to stand before him.

"And how are we feeling today?" he asked. "Ready at last for a big Babylonian breakfast?"

"No thanks," said Belteshazzar. "I'm feeling fine."

"Me too," said Shadrach.

"Couldn't be better," added Meshach.

"Healthy and happy and fit!" chirped Abednego.

And all the servants and guards and other officials had to agree.

"The king will be pleased," one of them said. "You have done a brilliant job with these newcomers, Ashpenaz. They are in better shape than any of the other boys!"

"And what about your friend?" Ashpenaz asked. "Surely he is better still?"

"No, he's not," said Belteshazzar. "He's been up all night. As sick as a dog."

And so it was that Belteshazzar, Shadrach, Meshach, and Abednego were blessed by the God they would not forget. They became famous for their intelligence, their wisdom, and their courage.

And Nigel?

All he got was a really bad tummy.

The Lion's Version

Daniel in the Lions' Den

It's tough being a lion. And I'm not lion.

Lion? Get it? Lyin'. Sorry.

That's the problem. Nobody expects a lion to have a sense of humour. We're supposed to be fierce and proud and obsessed with tearing things to bits. And, fair enough, some lions are.

Take my sister, for example. She'd sooner bite the head off a bunny than look at it. You just don't mess with her. Particularly at dinner time.

But me? I'm just put together differently, I guess. I'll let the odd bunny past. No problem. Antelopes, just the same. Sure, I like a good meal now and then.

Who doesn't? Circle of life and all that. But I'm not looking to devour everyone in the room or kill the first thing that moves. I'd rather just lie in the sun and enjoy the moment.

That's what I was doing, in fact, when they dropped this old guy into my living space.

When I say "living space", I mean the place where my sister and I hang out. It's not in the wild as it used to be when we were cubs. It's smaller. There's an "outside" bit with rocks to lie on and an "inside" bit that's covered, for when it rains. A den.

And when I say "they", I mean the men who took us from the wild to this place and who drop food down into our living space from time to time.

My sister hates this arrangement. As I said, she enjoys the hunting thing and is generally quite grumpy anyway. Me? I love it! Free food. Regular naps. What more could a lion ask for?

Anyway, this old guy dropped down into the den one day, and at first I wasn't quite sure what to do.

My sister, of course, was all roar and fang and claw.

"Calm down," I told her. "Let's think this thing through."

"What's to think about?" she growled. "He dropped down. He's dinner!"

All instinct, my sister. All the time.

"But look at him," I said. "There's no meat on

those bones. What kind of dinner is that? I think this is a mistake. I say he's actually one of the dinner-droppers and that he FELL down. And if we eat him, we might make the other dinner-droppers mad."

"So?" she grunted.

"So," I argued, "they might not feed us again. Not if we've eaten one of them."

"But how do we find out?" she replied. "It's not as if we can ask them."

"We wait," I said, "and see if they come back for him. Look, he's on his knees. He's staring up in the air. And he's saying something. Maybe he's calling for help."

"But I'm hungry," she grumbled.

"You're always hungry," I grumbled back. "How about we wait until it's dark? If they don't come back by then, we'll know that they meant to feed him to us. And, fine, you can eat whatever meat you can pick off those bones of his."

Then I went back to my rock and fell asleep.

When I woke up, the sun was setting, the old guy was still kneeling, and my sister was drooling.

"Any minute now," she smiled.

"Whatever," I shrugged. "There's been plenty of time for them to come back for him."

And then somebody else dropped in.

I say "dropped in". I suppose I really mean "appeared".

He wasn't there and then he was. Bit like a meerkat, popping up out of hole. But there was no hole. And he was bigger than a meerkat. Lots bigger.

My sister, of course, decided that he would make a much better dinner than the old guy in the corner. So she leaped in his direction, claws bared, fangs flashing. Big Mistake.

First, she flew right through him! I am not making this up. It was as if he was made of air. Whoosh!

"Might want to rethink this, Sis," I suggested. But the adrenalin was flowing. And the blood lust. She's an animal – what can I say?

So she leaped again. And this time, he was as solid as a rock – and she bounced off him with a whimper and a thud.

"Sis," I sighed, "leave it. You're not gonna eat that one."

"Then I'll have the old man," she growled.

"No, you won't," said the newcomer. And my sister and I just looked at each other.

"Did you hear that?" I whispered.

"I did," she whispered back.

"Not a man then," I said. "They can't understand us."

"What then?" she replied.

And our visitor smiled and said, "An angel."

It was, I must admit, a new concept to me. Not

man. Not lion. Not meerkat. So I asked him to explain.

"I am a servant of the Most High God," he said, "who is the Maker of All Things."

Now this I understood. In fact, I found it quite comforting. I would often lie on my rock, staring up into the sky. Clouds in the day. Stars at night. My sister thought I was lazy. But I was actually thinking. And one of the things I'd thought was, "This can't all be here by chance. Somebody must have made it." And here was the proof.

But my sister? She just grunted, "So what?"

"So," the angel answered, "I have been sent by the Maker of All Things to protect Daniel – the man over there."

"Because...?" I asked. I was on a roll, thinking-wise.

"Because he has followed the Maker faithfully, praying to him daily."

"Praying...?" I asked again.

"Talking to the Maker," the angel explained. "And, for that, a king called Darius, who rules this land, has said that he must die. And he has ordered his men to leave him here for you to eat."

"Sounds like a plan to me," grinned my sister.

"Wait a minute," I said. "This Darius wants him dead just because he talked to the Maker? I don't get it."

"To be fair," the angel explained, "the king does not want him to die. He was tricked into this by his advisors – men who are jealous of Daniel. They are the ones who want him dead."

"And they call us animals," I sighed. "We only kill to eat."

"And, speaking of eating…" added my sister.

"Yes, yes, I see the dilemma," said the angel. "You want to eat Daniel. I need to protect him. How about this? What if we wait until morning?"

"Morning?" moaned my sister.

"Wait until morning," the angel continued. "And I promise you the biggest meal you've ever had."

My sister looked sceptical. "The biggest? Really?"

"Really!" the angel grinned. "I promise."

"Say you'll wait, Sis," I whispered. "You've already tried to get past him. It's the only choice you've got."

"All right," she sighed, "Might as well go to sleep then." And she curled up into a ball.

I went back to my rock. And the angel? Who knows? He was awake the next morning when I woke up. My sister was awake, too, waiting for her breakfast. And so was somebody else.

"It's King Darius," the angel explained, as a head peeped over the edge of our den. And then the head said something.

"What's he going on about?" I asked.

"He wants to know if Daniel is still alive," the angel translated, while Daniel shouted and jumped up and down.

"I take it that means 'yes'," I chuckled.

"Good call," the angel chuckled in return. "And now the king is saying how pleased he is, and that

135

Daniel's god must be the true god if he could save him from a den of hungry lions."

"Yes. Hungry," my sister interrupted. "What about that promise of yours?"

"Hold on," said the angel. "Ah, yes, here it comes. King Darius says that Daniel will now be set free. Look, there's the rope. And there he goes. And – wait for it – the evil advisors who were jealous of Daniel will now be condemned to take his place. And here they come!"

My sister's eyes were as big as saucers, for the three men who dropped down into the den were the fattest three men either of us had ever seen!

"Lots of meat on those bones," I said.

"King's advisors eat well," nodded the angel.

"Breakfast time!" roared my sister. And, well, do you really want me to describe what happened next? Suffice to say that it was, as promised, the biggest meal she'd ever had.

"Farewell," said the angel.

"Fangs. Fangs a lot," I replied. "Get it? Fangs. Fanks. Thanks."

That's all right – the angel didn't laugh either. He just rolled his eyes and did his meerkat disappearing act. First he was there. Then he was gone. Back to the Maker of All Things.

And (heh heh) I'm not lion!

The New Testament

The Landlord's Version

The Shepherds and the Birth of Jesus

"Watch where you're stepping!" Avi's mum shouted as he sleepily slipped down the stairs.

"What?" the boy grunted. And then, "Why?"

"Ask your father," she grunted back. "And then maybe, once he's answered you, he'll get off his backside and give me a hand."

Avi's dad tipped his stool, leaned back against the wall, and grinned. "It was nothing, Son. Just a little party we had here last night."

"A little party?" said Avi's mum. "That's how you describe it?" Her voice was getting louder.

"A LITTLE PARTY?" And now she was shouting.

"OK, a right old knees-up!" he admitted.

"With…?" she added.

"With a load of shepherds," he smiled.

Avi scratched his head. "Shepherds? I didn't know you knew any shepherds."

"We most certainly do not know any shepherds!" Avi's mum grumbled. "Nobody in polite society knows any shepherds." She was glaring at his dad now. "NOBODY!"

"To be fair," he corrected her, "we actually do know some shepherds now. There was old Samuel. And young Elijah. And that little man with the crusty thing wrapped around his foot…"

"That WAS his foot!" Avi's mum muttered darkly. "And don't put that thing in your mouth!" she shouted at Avi's little sister, Hanna, who was sitting on the floor.

"Marble," said Hanna.

And Avi's mum stomped across the room and snatched it from her two-year-old fingers.

"Do you see what you have done?" she cried, waving the thing that was not a marble at Avi's dad.

"Calm down, dear," he shrugged. "A little sheep poo

141

never hurt anyone. Although," he continued, looking closer, "that might actually BE a marble."

Avi's mum stamped her foot. "I will not calm down. We are a respectable inn. Never in my wildest dreams did I imagine that I would be sweeping up after sheep in this dining room!"

"So how did the shepherds get here in the first place?" Avi asked.

"An excellent question!" Avi's mum replied. She was glaring at his dad again. "Shall I answer, darling, or would you like to?"

"They were happy," said Avi's dad. "They were running up and down the street, shouting about the good news that they wanted to share."

"That doesn't sound so bad," Avi shrugged.

"Really?" his mother sneered, digging a clump of wool out of Hanna's cheek. "Not so bad? Then why did Martha up at the Rook and Rock Badger slam the door on them? Why did Melchizedek blow out every lamp at the Hoof and Hippo?"

"Because they didn't want to hear the news?" guessed Avi.

"Because they were SHEPHERDS!" she shouted. "Filthy, stinking, flea-bitten, sheep-shifting shepherds! And nobody with any concern for their reputation," she was glaring at Avi's dad yet again, "lets a gang of shepherds into their establishment!"

"So what was the good news?" asked Avi, sheepishly.

"Craziness," grumbled his mum.

"Now that's a matter of opinion, dear," said his dad. "It seems that the shepherds had – how shall I put it – a run-in with some angels."

"Angels?" said Avi. "That does actually sound kind of crazy."

But Avi's dad wasn't giving up. "I'll admit it,"

he said. "It all sounded a little crazy to me, too. But I had a good sniff at them and none of them had even a hint of alcohol on their breath. They were sober. And I should know."

"So they met these angels…" said Avi. "And then…?"

"And then the angels told them something about the messiah," his dad went on.

"The messiah?" Avi asked.

"With the emphasis on mess," his mother sighed. "I'll never get this place clean! Hanna, do not stick that up your nose!"

"Yes, the messiah," his dad answered. "The special saviour that God promised to send our people to deliver us from our enemies."

"What did they say?" asked Avi.

"The angels told the shepherds that the messiah had been born. Here in Bethlehem. Last night. At an inn up the road."

Avi's mother rolled her eyes. "The Dog and Donkey, of all places. Biggest dump in town. As if God would let the messiah be born there!"

"Well, that's what the angels said," his dad continued. "And that's where the shepherds went after the angels sang a song."

"A song?" said Avi.

"Yeah. Something about peace on earth and goodwill to men. The shepherds sang it for me. It was catchy."

"It was crazy!" Avi's mum countered. "Songs blaring. Sheep bleating. Not one of them in tune!"

"What, the sheep?" asked Avi.

"No, the shepherds!" shouted his mum. "I'm surprised you got any sleep at all."

"The boy was probably counting sheep," joked Avi's dad. But his mum was not smiling.

"Sorry," he muttered. "Anyway, the shepherds said that they went up to the inn and, sure enough, there in the cowshed – out the back – they found a man and a woman and a newborn baby."

"And the baby was lying where?" Avi's mother huffed. "Go on, tell him."

"In the feed trough," said Avi's dad.

"The feed trough?" said Avi. "Really?"

"Really!" nodded his mum. "So these shepherds said. Now you tell me – what kind of god sends his special long-awaited saviour to earth and gives him to a family who sticks him, not one day old, in a feed trough?"

"The angels said it was a sign," his dad protested, "so that the shepherds would know they were at the right place."

"Furthermore," his mum went on, "what kind of god sends this special long-awaited saviour to be born in the back of a run-down inn, while there are at least three respectable establishments in the same town from which to choose?"

"Now, dear," said Avi's dad, "there's no need to take this personally."

"And finally," she said finally, "what kind of god sends an angelic choir to announce the birth of his long-awaited saviour to a filthy, flea-infested bunch of tone deaf shepherds? Hanna, I will not say it again, take that out of your mouth!"

"More marble," said Hanna.

"I'll tell you what kind of god!" she shouted. "A god for crazy people. Crazy unwashed people who have spent far too many lonely nights on the hills outside this city!"

Then she crossed her arms and stamped one foot and waited for a response.

"D'you want to go up to the Dog and Donkey to have a look?" said Avi.

"I was hoping you'd ask," grinned his dad.

"And now you have both gone crazy, too," sighed his mum. "Well, if you must go, why don't you take your sister with you? She's already had her daily ration of sheep poo. A nap in a feed trough would probably suit her just right!"

"OK, Mum," Avi chuckled as he disappeared out of the door.

"We'll be right back," said his dad, scooping up Hanna. "We won't be long. And when we get back," he added, "we'll help you clean up this place. Promise."

Avi's mum rolled her eyes. "Now that really would be good news."

The Brother's Version

The Wedding at Cana

Gehazi's Aunt Miriam grabbed his face with her two pudgy hands and placed her equally pudgy lips on his forehead. "Your sister is such a beautiful bride!" she beamed. "You should be proud. And what a handsome young man you are!"

The kiss left two fat wet spots. It was all he could do to keep himself from wiping them away.

"Thanks, Aunt," he said with as much enthusiasm as he could muster. Which wasn't much enthusiasm, to be honest, seeing as she was probably the twentieth aunt who had done much the same thing.

And then one of the servants asked her if she wanted some wine. And she said, "Yes, of course, how delightful." And Gehazi was mercifully left on his own again.

Weddings. For a boy with five big sisters and only two of them already married, weddings were torture. Torture then. Torture now. Torture yet to come.

The only thing that made this particular wedding bearable was that Anna, the bride, was his favourite sister and Adam, the bridegroom, was just about the nicest guy he'd ever met.

His other sisters' husbands hardly knew he existed. But Adam treated him almost as if he was one of his own brothers. Which meant a lot to a boy who had no brothers of his own.

So Gehazi stood there and smiled and put up with the kisses and the head-patting and the relatives who couldn't even remember his name.

"Psst," came a whisper from the other side of the doorway. "Over here." And then there was his cousin, Shem.

"Go away," Gehazi whispered back. "I'm busy. I don't want to get in trouble."

Shem crept through the doorway. The whisper got louder. "Who said anything about getting into trouble?"

Gehazi rolled his eyes. "You're here. There will be trouble. There always is."

Shem sniggered. "Yeah, but you've got to admit it – I always have fun. Like when I set the donkey loose at MY sister's wedding."

Gehazi grinned. "Yes, it was pretty good when it wandered into the reception and knocked over the pudding."

"On Uncle Ezra!" Shem chuckled. "Classic!"

"But you hate your sister," Gehazi reminded him.

"Hate?" Shem chuckled again. "No, I don't!

I just think she's stuck-up and knows it all and is her daddy's little princess and looks like a pig. But I don't hate her."

"Well, I like my sister," said Gehazi. "And I don't want to spoil her wedding. So no trouble, OK?"

"No trouble," Shem shrugged. "But that doesn't mean that we can't sneak out the back for a while and find something more interesting to do."

"I don't know…" Gehazi hesitated. And then another aunt – Aunt Agatha – grabbed his face.

Gehazi held his breath. Shem cringed.

And when another fat slobbery kiss had ended, Aunt Agatha looked at Shem and shook her finger in his direction. "Don't think YOU'LL be getting one of those," she grunted. "Not after that prank you played at your uncle's funeral."

Then she stamped away. And Gehazi exhaled at last.

"Terrible breath," noted Shem.

"Like a rotting corpse," agreed Gehazi. "So what happened at the funeral?"

Shem smiled. "You remember that little high pitched sneezy sound that Uncle Judah used to make? Well, at the funeral, I hid behind the coffin, and when Aunt Death-Breath walked by, I sort of did an impersonation of it."

"And…" asked Gehazi.

"And she nearly died, too," Shem grinned. "I can't

help it if people don't have a sense of humour."

"That's what I mean," Gehazi sighed. "You think 'funny'. Everybody else thinks 'trouble'."

"Oh, c'mon," Shem pleaded. "Look, Aunt Hilda is coming this way. She's got that thing on her face. That thing that looks like a camel. You don't really want that thing touching you, do you?"

"Point taken," Gehazi nodded. And the two of them took off in the direction of the kitchen.

"Not much going on back here," observed Gehazi as several servants scurried past them.

"Not much that's interesting anyway," Shem sighed. And then he peeped around the corner into a storage area and his eyes lit up. "You have got to see this melon!" he grinned.

"There are plenty of melons out there on the tables," said Gehazi, looking around. He was starting to get a little nervous.

"Not like this melon," said Shem, steering his cousin around the corner and pointing up to a shelf. "LOOK!"

So Gehazi looked. And when he did, he couldn't help but laugh.

"It's amazing, isn't it?" laughed Shem as well. "Looks just like the head of our dear departed Uncle Judah! I'm going to climb up there and grab that melon – and set it on Aunt Death-Breath's table when she isn't looking."

"I don't know…" Gehazi hesitated. "I told you I don't want to spoil the wedding."

"It won't spoil anything!" Shem argued. "Come on, give me a boost."

Gehazi was still hesitant. "I just think that maybe…"

"All right then," grunted Shem. "I'll do it myself." And he stepped up onto the edge of a tall jar of wine.

"Careful," warned Gehazi.

"I'll be fine," Shem smiled, reaching for the melon.

But as he grabbed the melon, he lost his balance. And the jar tipped. And as it fell, it tipped into another jar. Which tipped into another. And by the time Shem hit the floor, it was covered in wine.

"I did not expect that," said Shem, clutching the melon. "Oh, and I think I hear my mum calling. See you, Cuz."

And he dashed out of the storage area, leaving Gehazi alone with a pile of broken jars and a pool of wine.

He wasn't alone for long, though.

A servant rounded the corner and when he saw the mess, he cried, "What have you done?"

"Nothing," Gehazi pleaded. "Nothing. It wasn't me!"

"Well, it was somebody," said the servant. "And you're the only one standing there. The last time I left this room, it was filled with wine. And now... you have somehow managed to break every jar! This is all we had!"

"But it wasn't me!" Gehazi said again. And then he realized. It didn't really matter. The wine was gone. That was what mattered. And his sister's wedding was ruined!

Another minute and another head popped around

the corner. Gehazi cringed. Of all the people in the wedding, it had to be… Aunt Agatha.

"WHAT is going on in here?" she demanded. And Gehazi and the servant both started talking at once.

Aunt Agatha held up one hand to silence them. She looked at the mess and at the boy and at the servant. Then she looked especially hard at the small purple footprints exiting the room.

"There is no need to explain," she said. "You," she continued, pointing at the servant, "need to clean this place up. And you," she went on, looking straight at Gehazi, "need to be careful of the company you keep."

Just then, one more head peeped around the corner.

"Mary, my dear," Aunt Agatha sighed, "there appears to have been a bit of an… accident back here. It seems we've run out of wine."

"And now my sister's wedding is ruined!" added Gehazi, wiping one eye with the back of his hand.

Mary looked around the room. Then she put a hand on Aunt Agatha's shoulder. "I just might be able to help," she said calmly. "Or rather, my son might. I'll have a word with him. Leave it to me." And she slipped away.

"Who was that?" asked Gehazi.

"An old friend. From Nazareth," said Aunt Agatha. "She's here with her son, Jesus."

"Does he sell wine?" Gehazi wondered out loud.

"No," answered his aunt. "He's a rabbi. Can't imagine how he could help. Bit of a mystery, actually. But then, I like a good mystery!" And her eyes twinkled mischievously. "Now let's get you cleaned up."

When they emerged from the storage room, the servant had not yet returned to clear up the mess.

And when Aunt Agatha saw him chatting excitedly with all the other servants, she shouted, "I thought I told you to clean up that room!"

"Sorry. Very sorry," the servant apologized. "I was on my way to do it. And then another lady stopped me and told me to go and talk to her son. She said that he would be able to find us some more wine."

"That must have been your friend," said Gehazi to his aunt.

"Exactly what I was thinking," she nodded. The twinkle was back in her eye. "And what did he tell you?" she asked the servant.

"The man said that we should pour water into these six stone jars."

"Very curious," said Aunt Agatha. "And…?"

"So we did," answered the servant.

"And…?" said Aunt Agatha again.

"And you can taste it for yourself!" said another servant, dipping a cup into the jar and handing it to her.

Aunt Agatha took a sip from the cup and her eyes popped wide open.

"What is it?" asked Gehazi.

"It's wine! And not just any wine, but probably the best I've ever tasted."

"But how?" asked Gehazi. "How did Jesus do it?"

"Who knows?" said Aunt Agatha. "And who cares? Your sister's wedding has been saved. That's all that matters." Then she dipped her cup back into the jar and had another drink. "And you boys had better start passing this around before I finish it all."

Gehazi watched as the wine went around the

room – and as each and every guest reacted as his aunt had. He went over to talk to his sister and her husband, but was stopped by the master of the banquet. To Gehazi's surprise, the man started shaking his new brother-in-law by the hand.

"Sir," the man said, "most hosts serve their best wine first, but you have saved the best until last!"

And then Gehazi heard a scream from the other side of the hall.

"Oh no!" he thought. "I forgot to warn Aunt Agatha about the Uncle Judah Melon Head."

He raced across the room, and that's when he saw it. The scream had not come from Aunt Agatha at all. It had come from his cousin Shem. His aunt had a tight grip on the boy's ear and was dragging him toward the storage room.

"Please, Aunt, let go!" he pleaded. "It was only a bit of fun."

"And I have a bit of fun for you!" she answered. "Helping to clear up the mess you made."

"Cuz! Cuz!" he called to Gehazi. "Give me a hand here!"

"Sorry," Gehazi grinned, "got to go. I think I hear my mum calling."

Sonny's Version

Jesus and the Sons of Zebedee

Abraham ben Abraham hated cats.

This was not unusual for his time. In the first century in Galilee, which was when and where Abraham ben Abraham lived, everybody hated cats.

They didn't curl up on people's cushions. They didn't get fed from brightly coloured bowls. And nobody kept them as pets.

They got ignored. Or shouted at. Or kicked across the street. And that was by people who simply didn't like them. Not by people like Abraham ben Abraham who despised their very existence.

The reason that Abraham ben Abraham hated cats, along with his father, and his father's father (who were all called Abraham ben Abraham), is that he was a fisherman. And for a fisherman, fish equals profit. The more fish, the more profit. The fewer fish, the less profit.

And because cats eat fish and have no qualms about pinching them from the nets of hard-working fishermen, fish plus cat equals less profit. So Abraham ben Abraham hated cats.

Abraham ben Abraham had a son. A son called Sonny. It was officially, of course, Abraham ben Abraham. But because "ben" means "son of", Sonny thought that "Sonny" would make a nice nickname – and that it would also annoy his father.

Annoying his father was not Sonny's only goal in life, but it was at the top of the list. At position number one, actually. He was eleven – nearly a man by the standards of his day – and determined not to be ruled by his father's expectations. It will therefore come as no surprise that the number two goal in Sonny's life was to have a cat.

A particular cat, as it happens. A scruffy, thin, ginger cat with a tail shaped like a question mark. A cat called Pat.

Sonny did not know this was the cat's name, of course, because in first-century Galilee, nobody called cats names. Well, they did. They called them names like "Getlost" or "Goaway" or "Thievinglittleswine".

Which is why the cats came up with names of their own. Nicer names, on the whole. Names like "Tickle". Or "Scratch". Or "Pat".

And so it was that one foggy morning, Abraham ben Abraham and Sonny and Pat the cat made their way, each in his own way, to a fishing boat, moored at the Sea of Galilee.

Abraham ben Abraham's "way" could be described as "completely cheesed off with the world". On this particular morning, Abraham ben Abraham was completely cheesed off with his chief competitors – a pair of brothers called James and John ben Zebedee.

"Flippin' unfair advantage," he muttered. "Blinkin' luck," he grumbled.

Sonny had heard it all before and had managed to work out that it had to do with the brothers sharing a rather nice boat with their father – the "Zebedee" bit of "ben Zebedee".

He couldn't have cared less, as it happens, which was his "way". And he managed to look as uninterested as possible whenever his father's rants grew loudest. Which annoyed Abraham ben Abraham no end (see Sonny's number one goal).

Pat's "way" was to sniff around fishing boats, which was what he was doing as Abraham ben Abraham and Sonny arrived.

"Getlost… youthievinglittleswine!" shouted Abraham ben Abraham, using what the cat assumed were the man's first and last names for him. So he did, straightening his tail into an exclamation mark and scampering away.

Abraham ben Abraham climbed into the boat and set about doing a variety of "setting out to sea" tasks.

Sonny wasn't much interested in such things. But seeing as his survival depended on knowing what to do in a boat, he forced himself to pay attention.

There was some business

about the mast. And the sail. And the oars. And the nets. Which were inevitably tangled. So it fell to him to untangle them. Which gave him the opportunity to drag them off the boat and onto the shore. Which meant that he could look for Pat.

This, as it turned out, was not difficult. Not nearly as difficult as straightening out a tangled net, at any rate.

Pat was hiding under the edge of the boat. And when Sonny reached into the bag that he carried around his neck and produced a fish head, Pat's tail and whiskers and taste buds rose to attention.

So Sonny laid the fish head beside the net he was straightening. Abraham ben Abraham carried on with his set of seafaring tasks. Pat the cat matched the question mark in his head to the question mark shape that was now his tail and slowly crept out from under the boat toward the tasty fishy treat. And everyone else launched their boats into the sea and set sail. And that included James and John, the sons of Zebedee.

"Blast!" shouted Abraham ben Abraham when he caught sight of the brothers' boat. Then he shouted again. "Where's that flippin' net?"

"Right here!" Sonny shouted back, dragging it in its newly untangled state onto the boat.

"They've got a head start!" he fumed. "Let's get a move on!"

So they did. All that morning and into the early part of the afternoon. And what did they catch?

"Nothing!" grumbled Abraham ben Abraham. "Not a flipper, not a fin, not a...."

"Fing!" added Sonny, trying to sound just that little bit "street" – a habit which annoyed his father nearly as much as sons of Zebedee and cats.

And, speaking of cats, what had happened to Pat?

The answer is quite simple. While everyone else was preparing their boats, Sonny managed to lure the cat closer and closer to him by producing more and more fish heads. And eventually, he managed to lure the cat into the bag itself, where an even greater quantity of fish heads resided. I say "resided". I actually mean "lay there, dead and disjointed from their bodies".

So the cat was literally in the bag. On board the boat. Chewing on fish heads.

I know this seems improbable. All I can say is

that it was a reasonably large bag. And an unusually small cat. And that the fish heads were incredibly delicious. So Pat was willing to "go along for the ride", so to speak – and did, in fact, end up going along for the ride.

As it happens, the ride came to an abrupt end, within shouting distance of the sons of Zebedee.

Shouting was what Abraham ben Abraham was inclined to do whenever he was near the brothers Zebedee. But he was concerned that shouting on this occasion would give rise to the inevitable fisherman's question, "Caught anything yet?"

And since the answer to that question had already been established as "not a flipper, not a fin, not a fing", he didn't want to embarrass himself in front of his chief competitors.

He needn't have worried. James and John had no such qualms. They had never thought of Abraham ben Abraham as their chief competitor. In fact, they barely knew he existed.

This would have brought no comfort to Abraham ben

Abraham. What did bring him comfort, though, was when they shouted back, "No luck today, mate. Haven't caught a thing."

At that point, something unusual happened. Abraham ben Abraham smiled.

And Sonny? Sonny was shocked. For that was the very first time he had ever seen a smile on his father's face.

The fact that it was not a nice smile made little difference to the boy. The fact that the smile had arisen from the complete failure of two fellow fishermen to provide for their families that day was  of little concern. Sonny had seen his father smile. In fact, so struck was he by the moment that he very nearly told Abraham ben Abraham about the cat.

But just as he opened his mouth, another unusual thing happened.

Jesus arrived in a boat with Simon, a friend of James and John. He told Simon where to cast his net. Simon did so and hauled in a great catch of fish. Then he called for the sons of Zebedee to help him drag it in, for it was too much for just one boat!

And just as quickly as it had arrived, the smile disappeared from Abraham ben Abraham's face.

Sonny watched it all, amazed. And so he said, quite understandably, "That's unbelievable! That's incredible! That's a miracle!"

Which, in fact, it was.

A point that was not lost on Abraham ben Abraham. "Flippin' sons of Zebedee!" he muttered. "Blinkin' divine intervention!" he moaned.

And, cursing and grumbling, he set sail for home.

Sonny kept his mouth shut all the way. But the cat, unaware of anything but the delights of fish heads, began to purr. The sound of that purr was masked by the washing of the waves against the boat. Until, that is, the vessel bumped with a thump against the shore. And the bag rolled forward. And the purr turned into a noisy meow.

"That's a cat!" shouted Abraham ben Abraham. "A cat in your bag. On my boat!"

And before Sonny could move, his father grabbed the boy's arm with one hand, snatched the bag off the deck with the other, and held it in the air.

Pat the cat squirmed and twisted and yowled.

Sonny begged and pleaded.

"It's been an awful day," sneered Abraham ben Abraham. "But now, at least, there is one thing that will make me happy." And he dangled the bag over the water and laughed the nastiest of nasty cat-drowning laughs.

And then a third unusual thing happened.

James and John and Simon and his brother
Andrew all came walking by.

"We're done with fishing," they announced. "We're
following Jesus now."

"And you, you holding that bag!" shouted John.
"Why don't you have our catch for the day?"

Abraham ben Abraham turned and walked to the end of the boat, letting go of Sonny's arm and dropping the bag on the deck as he went.

"What… what did you say?" he stammered.

"You can have our fish," said John. "They're all yours, mate."

And suddenly the smile was back. And fish, like numbers – indeed, fish-shaped numbers – added themselves up in Abraham ben Abraham's brain. Fish upon fish upon fish upon fish upon profit!

"Did you hear that, boy?" he shouted. "It IS a miracle! A miracle after all!"

And, forgetting everything else, including the cat, he raced off to count his fish.

But Sonny sat down and opened up the bag. He would not have been surprised if the cat was dead. He would not have been surprised if the cat had bolted. He was surprised, however, when somewhat miraculously the cat crept slowly out of the bag and rubbed itself up against his leg.

So he did what you do when a cat does that.

He reached out his hand. And gave him a pat.

The Apprentice's Version

Jesus Heals a Man Lowered Through a Roof

Uncle Saul looked down through the hole and shook his bald head. "Lotta damage here," he grunted. And he sucked a big breath in through his teeth. "Big job. Big, big job. This is gonna cost you."

The man who owned the house looked up through the hole and shook his head as well. "I was afraid of that," he sighed. "Well, it's got to be done. So get on with it – as quick as you can."

And he trudged out of the house and down the street.

"As quick as you can. Right," muttered Uncle

Saul. "Like I've got nothing else to do."

"But you don't, Uncle Saul," I said. "You were telling me just yesterday that the work had dried up."

"That was yesterday!" he snapped. "Today. Today there are deals in the works. Opportunities to be taken advantage of. You've got a lot to learn about business, boy!"

I did, I guess. I was just his apprentice, after all. Tagging along to learn the trade. But I was still confused. Unless Uncle Saul had somehow managed to do a deal in his sleep, I couldn't see how anything had changed from the night before.

"What I want to know," he grumbled, searching through his bag for a measuring line, "is how this happened in the first place."

"I know," I offered. "My friend Andrew told me. Some men did it."

"Men? What, like robbers?" he asked. "It's not the quietest way to break into a place."

"No, no, not robbers," I said. "Just four men."

"Vandals then?" he grunted. "I hate vandals. I say hate… I mean, they're good for business – don't get me wrong. But to tear somebody's roof up just out of spite – that's sick." Then he handed me the end of the line and added, "Hold this. Don't let go."

"I don't think they were vandals either," I said, wrapping the end of the line around my finger, so it wouldn't slip. "But they did have a sick friend."

Uncle Saul paused. "Wait. Wait," he said. "You're telling me that these four guys came up here to vandalize this roof and that they brought their sick friend along just for the fun of it. Now that really is sick!"

"They weren't vandals," I sighed. "That's what YOU said. They were just trying to get their friend into the house."

"And the front door was too much trouble?" he grumbled.

"The front door was blocked," I replied.

"Oh? So if Mr Get-It-Done-Yesterday had simply hired me to fix his door in the first place, he wouldn't be looking at a big bill today. Typical!"

"It wasn't blocked because it was broken," I sighed. "It was blocked because the house was full of people!"

"Sick people?"

"Some of them, yeah, I guess. They were here to see Jesus."

"Jesus the one-eyed spear-sharpener?" he exclaimed. "What did they want to see him for?"

"No, a different Jesus. Jesus the rabbi," I replied.

"Never heard of him," he grunted, letting go of the line. "I think we've got enough tiles to do the job."

"Well, he's kind of famous," I explained.

"Don't have time for celebrities," Uncle Saul shrugged. "I'm a plain, ordinary businessman just trying to make a living. And you'll do well to do the same."

"That's fine," I said. "I'm just saying that he's the reason the four men brought their sick friend along. Because he heals people."

Uncle Saul set a pile of tiles down beside the hole and looked at me very seriously.

"Now, you listen to me, boy. There are lots of folks wandering about, claiming lots of things. They'll tell your future. They'll make it rain. They'll resuscitate your dead donkey. In my experience, most of them are crooks. If you want to make an honest living, stick to construction." And he pounded his fist so hard on the roof that one of the tiles fell through the hole and shattered on the floor below.

"Never mind," he shrugged. "We'll charge him for that one, too. You have to allow for a certain amount of breakage."

"I don't think Jesus is a crook," I answered. "Andrew didn't say anything about his asking for money."

"Oh no," Uncle Saul sneered. "But he doesn't mind encouraging the odd bit of roof-wrecking."

"I don't think he encouraged them to do it. They were just really desperate to get their friend healed."

"So they decided to drop him through a hole in the roof?" Uncle Saul sniggered. "Bet that made him feel better."

"They didn't drop him," I said. "They lowered him on a mat – with ropes tied to the four corners. At least that's what Andrew told me."

"And he knows this how?" asked Uncle Saul, all sceptical.

"Because he was in the room down there," I pointed.

Uncle Saul fitted the tiles together and slowly started to cover up the hole.

"So they lowered him into the room – and then what?"

"People got out of the way. And Jesus talked to him

– and that's when the really strange thing happened."

"Oh, like tearing up a roof and lowering a sick guy into a crowded room isn't strange enough?" he grunted.

"Not as strange as this," I said. "Jesus looked at the man and told him, 'Your sins are forgiven.'"

Uncle Saul dropped another tile. "What did I

tell you?" he shouted. "Religious wackos. If it's not money, it's power they're after. So this guy thinks he's God, does he? 'Cause only God can forgive sins."

"That's exactly what the priests said!" I replied. "Some of them were in the house and Andrew said that they were really angry."

"So they set this Jesus straight, did they?"

"Not exactly. No. Before they could do anything, Jesus asked this really weird question: 'Which is easier – to forgive a man's sins or to heal him so he can walk again?'"

"Neither of them's easy!" Uncle Saul snorted. "What kind of question is that?"

"A question Jesus answered himself," I said. "'To prove that I have the power and the right to do the one,' he argued, 'I'll do the other.'

"And he told the man on the mat to get up and walk."

"And…?" asked my uncle Saul, as if he was waiting for the punchline.

"And the man got up and walked!" I said.

Uncle Saul shook his head, as if he was going to take some convincing. "But it still could have been a set-up. The four guys. The sick man. Maybe they were all working for this Jesus character."

And that's when I shook my head. "Don't think so," I said. "The man on the mat – the one who couldn't walk – that was Andrew's dad."

Uncle Saul grunted, "Humph." He was good at grunting. Then he put the last tile in place, and the job was done.

"Don't you think that's amazing?" I asked. "It's like a miracle!"

"What's amazing," he grunted again as he put

away his tools, "is that we got this job done so quickly. And as for miracles, I'm just a plain ordinary businessman, trying to make a living.
Now pick up that toolbox and let's get going.
There are deals to be made. That's what you need to concentrate on, boy – not all this religious stuff."

So I picked up the toolbox and followed him down

off the roof. But I have to admit that I wasn't so sure about what he said – and I wondered, just for a minute, if Jesus could use an apprentice.

The Dead Boy's Version

Jesus Raises the Widow's Son

People always ask me two things: what was it like to die? And what was it like to come back to life again?

The first question is harder, in a way, because I didn't think I was going to die. I was ill. I had a fever. The shakes. That sort of thing. Don't even know where it came from really. It just happened. So I didn't really have any time to think about it.

I guess if I had, I might have been worried or afraid, or I might have thought about how unfair it was to die when I was only thirteen.

But I don't remember thinking any of those things.

I was hot and shaky, then I sort of fell asleep, and that was it. I just didn't wake up again.

I know how my mum felt. At least I know what she told me. She was the one who was worried. Mainly because my dad had died of a fever and she had seen the symptoms before. She didn't say anything, of course, because she didn't want to scare me. But she was scared. Really scared.

And she was the one who thought it was unfair. She'd already lost her husband, and now it looked as if she might lose her son. So she had a word with God. That's what she told me. And she explained to him how wrong she thought it would be.

I died, of course. And she said that she wasn't just sad. She was angry, too. Angry at God for not making me well. And she was even angry at the friends and relatives who came to pay their respects – angry that they still had sons and husbands to bring with them.

I don't think she said anything to them. I mean, they've never said anything to me about that. But she was angry, I know that.

I think she was also angry that she didn't have any money to pay for the funeral and that she had to rely on those same friends and relatives to help her out. You'd think she would have been pleased that they were there for her. But I think it was a pride thing. Without a husband, she was already poor.

And without a son, well, she would pretty much have to depend on charity for the rest of her life. It's not how you plan for things to work out, is it?

Anyway, there she was in the funeral procession – angry and sad and poor and hopeless, all at the same time. And I was there, too – obviously – bouncing around in my open coffin as my uncles and cousins carried me to my grave. There was a huge crowd –

I guess they felt really sorry for my mum. And then all of a sudden, this rabbi called Jesus appeared out of nowhere, walked up to my mum, and said, "Don't cry."

Now, I don't know about you, but I don't think that's the first thing I would say to someone at a funeral. Particularly a total stranger. I think I would say something like "I'm sorry" or "What a shame", or maybe I'd just say nothing at all. But "Don't cry"? Don't be ridiculous!

That's exactly how my mum felt. At least that's what she told me. She didn't know whether to ignore him or spit at him or laugh at him. Or maybe just cry even harder. What she felt like doing was smacking him right across his rabbi face. But instead, she just looked down at the ground and said nothing.

You think that would have stopped the rabbi – dropped the hint that she didn't really want him there; that his comment wasn't exactly right for the occasion.

But no, he just kept going. He walked right up to my coffin and put his hand on it, as if he wanted the procession to stop.

Well, it stopped all right, mainly because everyone was so offended by what he'd done. I mean, what right did he have to burst into a funeral and disrupt everything? My mum told me that there was a lot of moaning and muttering at that moment. A bit of

shouting and swearing, too. And apparently, someone had to grab hold of Aaron, our next-door neighbour, to keep him from doing what my mum had only thought of doing – and more.

So the funeral was just about wrecked. And that's when I more or less came back into the picture.

You know how it is when you're really, really tired, and you fall asleep, and you sleep so soundly that the next thing you know, it's morning and you're awake again? As if no time at all has passed?

Well, that's how it was. Out of nowhere, I heard these words: "Young man, I say to you: get up!"

So I did. And seeing as I didn't actually realize that I was dead, it did sort of feel just like I was getting up. Nothing special. Nothing unusual.
I just opened my eyes and sat up.

Which was, of course, extremely unusual for the people who were attending the funeral!

The swearing turned to swooning. The shouting turned to screaming. And our neighbour Aaron dropped his fists and then fainted and dropped to the ground. It's safe to say that no one in Nain had ever seen anything like this before.

I was obviously shocked as well. What was I doing in a coffin? That was the first thing I wanted to know. But when my mum grabbed me and hugged me and started kissing me and telling me how glad she was to have me back, it became apparent that I had missed a pretty significant event in my life (so to speak).

She hugged Jesus as well, of course, and had plenty to say to him after that – how grateful she was, how amazed she was, how relieved she was, how good it was of God to finally answer her prayers. That sort of thing.

I got a lot of other hugs, too. Well, eventually. Lots of folks were just a little hesitant about putting their arms around someone who had been a corpse just a few minutes earlier. But they got over it, I guess, and in the end, I stepped out of my coffin and walked away from my funeral. And there aren't many people who can say that.

Sad to say, my mum passed away a couple of days ago. We talked a lot before she died and everything was good. She was so happy and so glad that I could be there to hold her hand. So grateful that she wasn't alone. I asked her if she wanted me to try to find Jesus for her, but she said, "No, one person raised from the dead is probably more than any family should expect. And if it had to be anyone," she said, "I'm glad that it was you."

So I'm off to the funeral now. I'm sad. But I'm also sort of glad, in a way. Not just that Jesus brought me back to life, but that, in another way, he brought her back to life, too. I'm not really expecting him to turn up, but who knows? I think I'll keep an eye out for strangers, just in case.

The Swineherd's Version

Jesus Heals a Man with Demons

My dad and I walked into the room and sat down. The man on the other side of the table looked very serious.

He didn't speak to us at first. I looked at my dad. My dad looked at me. I shuffled my feet. He folded and unfolded his hands. Neither of us knew what to expect.

Finally, the man smiled. But I wouldn't say that it was a friendly smile, exactly. More like something he was supposed to do.

"Now, then," he said. "My name is Mr Balak.

189

And I work for the Ten Towns Mutual Assurance Company. And you are… Farmer Swine?"

"That's right," my dad nodded.

"And this is…?" he asked, looking at me.

"My son. Swine Junior. He was there, on the day. The day of the attack."

"Yes. Well," said Mr Balak, "that is why we are here, isn't it? Because of what you call the 'attack'."

"I've already told the other man everything that happened," said my dad, defensively. "It was an attack. My pigs were killed. I don't know what else there is to say."

"Let's go over the details of the case," said Mr Balak. "And then, perhaps, you will understand why I have called this meeting."

Dad was sweating. He always sweated when he was nervous. "Sweated like a pig." That's what he'd always say. And given his job and our name, that was funny. But it wasn't funny now.

Mr Balak cleared his throat and began:

"As I understand it, you say that your entire herd of pigs plunged off a hill, at the edge of your property, into the sea, where they drowned. Furthermore, you say that this was the fault of a Jewish rabbi called Jesus, who was standing in a cemetery at the seaside below."

"That's right," my dad nodded. "That's exactly what happened."

"Hmm," muttered Mr Balak. "We shall see. Now then, your insurance policy does, indeed, cover acts of violence toward your herd. However, we have been unable to uncover any evidence that proves your claim to be true.

"Granted, some of your neighbours saw a rabbi and his followers at the seaside that day, but no one saw him approach your herd or attempt to disturb it in any way. He did not have a stick. There were no dogs present. Nothing, in fact, that could be used to chase even one pig off a cliff, much less an entire herd."

"I never said the man used a stick!" my dad replied. "It was unusual, what Jesus did, yes – but it was his fault. You talked to my witness, didn't you?"

Mr Balak nodded. And harrumphed. "Your witness? Yes, we did interview the witness that you suggested to us. And he did tell us a story similar to the one we heard from you.

"He explained that he was wandering among the tombs when Jesus and his disciples suddenly appeared on the shore. He described how he approached Jesus and how Jesus then cast a collection ('legion' is the word he used) of demons out of him and into your herd of pigs. And, according to him, that is why they then leaped to their watery doom."

"There you go," grinned my dad, slamming his hand on the table. "It was Jesus' fault! My witness saw him do it. Now all you need to do is pay me what my herd was worth, and my son and I will be on our way."

"Sadly, it is not as simple as that," replied Mr

Balak. And now there was nothing even approaching a smile on his face.

"I know you believe that this should have convinced us of the truth of your case. The only problem, Farmer Swine, is that you failed to tell us that your witness was a madman!

"Nutcase. Lunatic. Bonkers. That is how your neighbours describe this witness, Farmer Swine. According to our sources, he has spent much of the last few years of his life among the tombs. Naked – because of his illness. And chained – we can only guess – so that his mad rages would not prove harmful to himself or to others.

"While it is true that he seemed perfectly 'normal' during our interview, our experts have told us that madmen are very good at pretending to be normal. So the story he told us about Jesus and the demons could also have been a result of his madness. It certainly sounds 'mad' to me."

"But he's all right now," I blurted out. "Doesn't that count for something?"

They both turned and looked at me.

"Who is all right?" asked Mr Balak.

"The… the… madman," I answered. "He's not crazy any more. He doesn't have to be chained. He wears clothes. Doesn't that mean you should trust what he says?"

"Young man," Mr Balak replied, looking down his nose at me. "Unless you are an expert in mental diseases as well as a swineherd, what you say is a matter of opinion, and opinion only. The man was not in his right mind when this so-called attack occurred. So how can his evidence be trusted? And speaking of 'mad'…"

And here he turned his withering gaze upon my dad.

"Let's talk about your own failure to provide fencing at the edge of the cliff. Demons or no demons, a good strong fence would have stopped your pigs from their deadly plunge – and they would be alive, rooting and snorting happily today."

Mr Balak folded his arms across his chest.

"No, Farmer Swine, in the absence of any other witnesses, we are going to have to reject your claim. You are free, of course, to find this rabbi and sue him for damages in civil court. But we suspect that a judge would be as skeptical of your witness's account as we are.

"We are sorry for your loss. But you must understand that insurance fraud is common these days and costs everyone – company and customer alike. This is not to imply, in any way, that we suspect your motives. It is simply a sad fact that every claim must be dealt with thoroughly. And in your case, the facts do not add up. It is unfortunate that your pigs plunged from the cliff to their deaths. But we can see no connection between that event and any human action. In the end, we must chalk it up as an 'act of God' and leave it at that.

"If you have any further questions, do not hesitate to contact me at your convenience."

"So I don't get any money?" asked my dad.

"Not a fig, I'm afraid," replied Mr Balak. "As I think I have said clearly, your insurance policy covered an attack on your herd. And there simply was no attack."

"But… but… that was my whole living," my dad sighed. "What am I supposed to do now?"

"I'm afraid I have no answer for that," said Mr

Balak, rising from the table. "But I do have another appointment. So if you will excuse me…" And he headed for the door.

I couldn't do it. I couldn't hold it in any longer.

"What if there were another witness?" I asked. "Someone who wasn't crazy?" And now I was sweating, too.

Mr Balak turned and looked at me.

"What other witness?" he asked.

"Me," I mumbled.

"You?" said my dad. "But you were up on the hill with the pigs! That's what you told me. You tried to stop them, but they ran right past you. That's what you said. Are you saying that you have been lying to me all this time?"

"Yes," I whispered.

"Sorry," I whispered, too. "I knew you'd be angry if you found out. I thought you'd blame me for the pigs. But I don't think I could have stopped them, anyway."

"That is not the point, young man," said Mr Balak, returning to his seat. "The point is: where were you?"

"Down in the cemetery," I confessed. "With… Colin… you know… the madman." I said. "Except he's not mad anymore, he really isn't!"

"But he was mad THEN!" said my dad.

"Yes, I suppose so," I shrugged. "But I knew him,

sort of. Well, as well as you can know any crazy naked chained-up person. I was on the hill every day, watching the pigs. And he was down there in the cemetery, doing his crazy naked thing. And at first I was just curious, so I went down there, and he sort of screamed at me for a bit. So I started leaving him bits of my lunch, which he liked. And then we got to saying 'Hi' and 'How are you doing?' and then 'Well, must be off, lots to do.'"

"Your mother will go spare when she finds out!" my dad shouted again.

"That's why I never said anything. I didn't want you to worry. He was chained up. I kept my distance. Like I said, I'm sorry."

Mr Balak cleared his throat. "Leaving your family issues and returning to the point for a moment, what exactly did you see and hear, young man, when you were down in the cemetery?"

"Everything that Colin told you," I replied. "All right, I was hiding behind a tomb, because I didn't know who the people in the boat were. But I peeped out from time to time, and I heard it all! Jesus told the demons that were in Colin to go into our herd of pigs."

"And you are certain that there were demons in Colin because…"

"Because they kept screaming, 'Jesus, Son of God, don't torture us! Jesus, don't send us into the abyss!' Like I said, I heard everything. And it was really scary!"

My dad looked at Mr Balak. "So does this change anything?" he asked.

"There is a part of me," said Mr Balak, "that wants to be suspicious about this sudden turn of events. But there is another part of me that saw the look on your face when your son confessed that he was in the graveyard. A part that believes you were truly surprised. So I will give both you and he the benefit of the doubt. You will receive money to buy a replacement herd, Farmer Swine. But can I suggest that you use at least part of that fund to build yourself a sturdy fence?"

"And maybe hire myself a swineherd who doesn't have crazy friends," my dad added, looking at me.

"No worries, Dad," I said. "I'll never leave the herd again. Promise."

"I'd take his word for that," said Mr Balak. "After all, in the end, he did save your bacon." And he shook my hand and my dad's hand and smiled. A real smile this time.

My dad smiled, too. And why shouldn't he? The Swines had pigs again!

Hector's Version

Jairus' Daughter

I didn't even want the grapes. I just wanted to annoy Gad the Grump.

I wanted to see his red grumpy face and watch him shake his grumpy fist. So I waited for a second, waving the grapes in the air. And when he finally squeezed himself out from behind his market stall, that's when I bolted.

There's this old Greek story about a tortoise and a hare. And I was the hare, zipping between piles of robes and tables of pottery and cartloads of vegetables.

I stopped every now and then, just to see how far he'd come. But I knew the story and I wasn't going to end up short of the finish line. So I gave myself plenty of time to get back to our stall, tossing the grapes to some kids along the way.

And then I waited. Honestly, a tortoise would have been faster. And when he finally arrived, I was quietly rearranging our merchandise, as if I had been there all along.

"You stole… my… grapes," he huffed. "You… little… thief!"

"Don't know what you're talking about, Grump," I shrugged.

"You know… very… well," he puffed. "And… don't call… me that!"

"And why not?" asked Uncle Zeno, his hand suddenly on my shoulder. "You're the grumpiest market trader this side of Jerusalem."

(Which was particularly funny, seeing as Uncle Zeno was not exactly not grumpy.)

"And you're a worthless Greek," grunted Gad. "I don't even know why they let you set up your stall here."

"Because everyone loves a good deal," my uncle grinned. "Jews and Greeks alike. Not the rubbish you peddle."

"Well, it was good enough to steal," the Grump growled.

"I don't see any grapes," my uncle replied. "So why don't you waddle back to your stall and leave the boy alone?"

"May the Lord God curse you and your boy," Gad grunted as he turned to leave.

"Oooh, I'm quaking in my sandals!" mocked Uncle Zeno.

"Cursed by a god nobody has ever seen, with a name nobody is allowed to say."

Then he turned as well – and smacked me on the head.

"What was that for?" I moaned.

"For stealing grapes," he muttered. Then he grinned. "And for not saving any for me."

Xerxes chuckled. He was Uncle Zeno's slave.

"And what are you laughing at?" I grunted.

"The grape does not fall far from the vine," he replied.

I scratched my head. Xerxes was always talking in riddles.

Uncle Zeno smiled. "I think what our Persian friend means is that the odd bit of thievery is part of – what shall I call it? – our family tradition."

This I understood. Uncle Zeno could sell anything. But it wasn't always clear where his "stock" had come from. He would often disappear in the middle of the night – and a whole new range of goods would appear on the stall in the morning.

Today it was mostly leather stuff. And a few pieces of cheap jewellery.

Just then, the crowd started buzzing and Gad the Grump came our way again with an important-looking man and his family.

I heard someone at the next stall say "Jairus", but it didn't mean anything to me. What I did notice was the man's daughter. Jews and Greeks don't usually get along, so I thought she'd ignore me. But she didn't. She smiled!

"Don't pay him any attention," I heard the Grump say. "The boy's not quite right in the head."

Big fat liar. So I smiled back extra hard, just to annoy him.

"He's right, you know," said Uncle Zeno. "You're not right in the head. Not if you fancy that Jewish girl."

"Icch," I said, annoyed and embarrassed all at the same time. "I don't fancy her. She just seems nice. That's all."

"Well, that's a good thing," he nodded. "You see, Greek boys can only marry Jewish girls if they become Jews, too."

"So?" I grunted.

"So," he chuckled again, "that means you'd have to give up those pork sausages you like so much."

"Really?"

"Anyway,"

he continued, "you're far too young to be thinking of girls. What are you, eight?"

"I'm not thinking of girls!" I insisted.

"And he's ten," added Xerxes. "We've had him eight years. He was two when he came to us. Try to keep up."

"A slave who can add," sneered Uncle Zeno. "What a marvellous asset! I don't know what I'd do without you."

"I know," Xerxes muttered again. "The word 'disaster' comes to mind."

"Oh, that's right," Uncle Zeno replied. "Like the disastrous deal I made for you. What did I give? A couple of blankets and three mangy cats. How I miss them now!"

They were like an old married couple, those two. Always fighting. Always making up. But I was tired of the argument, so I interrupted, saying, "Do Jews really not eat pork then? Not at all?"

"My dear Hector," sighed Uncle Zeno, "people do the most ridiculous things in the name of their gods."

"Here we go," sighed Xerxes, rolling his eyes.

"Yes. Yes," Uncle Zeno sighed back. "I know it drives you crazy. But the boy must be taught. Warned against the nonsense that is at the heart of every religion."

"In your opinion," muttered Xerxes.

"In my opinion?" Uncle Zeno repeated in

exasperation. "This from a man who worships Mithra and believes that every living thing sprouted from the bowels of a cow!"

"The belly of a bull," Xerxes answered, wearily.

"Oh yes, that's much more sensible!" Uncle Zeno replied.

"Well, it's as sensible as what you Greeks believe," said Xerxes.

"Not this Greek," Uncle Zeno insisted. "The less intelligent among my people may still believe that Hermes and Zeus wander down to earth and play tricks on us mere mortals. But anyone with half a brain knows that those are just stories – meant to frighten or entertain or control."

And then he looked me straight in the eye. "The reality, my boy, is that there are no gods. There's no heaven up there. And nothing but earth beneath our feet. We're born. We live. We die. That's the end of it. And in the meantime," he winked as a customer cast his eye on a piece of jewellery, "we try to make just as much money as we can!"

Making money was my hope a couple of days later as I sneaked up to the Grump's stall. Uncle Zeno always said that it wasn't how much you could sell something for that counted. It was how much you had to pay for it in the first place. So I thought that if I could steal a few bits from Gad's stall, then whatever I sold them for would be profit!

I waited until there was a crowd. I waited until he was looking the other way.

Or so I thought. Because just as I grabbed for a particularly shiny trinket, a fat hand grabbed my wrist.

"Gotcha!" he sneered. And there's no telling what he would have done had some lady not rushed up to him in a panic.

"Have you heard?" she cried. "Jairus' daughter. She's dying!"

Shocked, he released his grip and I pulled free. But I did not run. "Jairus?" I asked. "The one who was with his daughter the other day?"

"Of course, you imbecile!" the Grump shouted. "She's his only child!"

"He's gone to the centre of town," the lady continued, "to ask Jesus to heal her."

And then the Grump just forgot about me. He picked himself up off his stool and lumbered after the lady.

And, keeping my distance, I followed them.

I know what Uncle Zeno would have said: "Gods. Healing power. Stupid."

But she'd smiled at me. And I guess I just hoped that somehow somebody could make her well. And that didn't seem stupid at all.

When we caught up with Jairus, there were loads of people around him, all hurrying… somewhere.

"Where are we going?" I asked.

"To Jairus' house," someone answered. "But they're saying it's too late."

And sure enough, when the crowd stopped at a big house, someone came rushing forward to meet Jairus. And when he had spoken, Jairus tore his robes and fell to the ground.

Everybody around me started shaking their heads and crying. And then, from the front of the crowd, I heard people laughing! Not nice laughing, though. Sneering, Grump-laughing.

I crept through the crowd. And that's when I found out what the laughing was about.

"Jesus says she's only sleeping," someone sniggered.

"Some prophet he turned out to be," joked someone else.

"The mourners are here, for heaven's sake," sighed another voice. "The girl's dead!"

Uncle Zeno would have had a thing or two to add to that conversation. But I was really sad. The girl was dead. And I'd never even said "hi" to her.

So I pushed my way out of the crowd and wandered around the back side of the house, kicking stones and thinking about what Uncle Zeno had said. How we're born and we live and we die – and that's that. And how it didn't seem fair, somehow, that she'd only lived for a little while.

And then I heard something – something from the top of the house. I stepped back to get a better view and just managed to see the head of somebody in the window. It was Jairus. And standing next to him was another man – who I guessed was the Jesus everyone had been laughing about.

He was smiling, which seemed strange. And then his head disappeared, as if he was bending down. And the next thing I knew, there was another head in the window. The girl. Alive. With her arms wrapped around her father's neck! And he was crying. And she was crying. And I think I was crying, too.

She looked out the window. She looked right at me. And I wiped my eyes with the back of my hand and I waved.

And she waved back.

And then I ran. I don't know why. Maybe because I didn't want her to see me crying. Or because I just didn't know what else to do.

But Uncle Zeno knew. Or at least he had a theory, once I'd told him what had happened.

"It's very clear to me," he grinned. "You ran, my boy, because you suddenly remembered that doing anything else could be very bad news for your pork intake."

I didn't think that was the case, but I laughed anyway. And Xerxes laughed, too. And then he looked very seriously at Uncle Zeno and asked, "Do you doubt the power of God now?"

And Uncle Zeno just kept grinning. "I have no doubts," he began. "No doubts that this Jesus made a very lucky guess. The girl was obviously just sleeping. And he woke her up. Doesn't take a god to do that."

But I wasn't so sure.

"Maybe not," I thought. "But maybe… just maybe… well." It didn't seem like the right time to get into it.

And besides, Gad the Grump would still be on the other side of town. Which meant that it was the perfect time to help myself to a little more of his merchandise!

The Professional Mourner's Version

Jesus Raises the Dead

I'd never heard such wailing in my life. Which is saying something, really, seeing as wailing was my job. Or would have been, one day. I was an apprentice, you see, at Lamentations Limited, the nation's most famous firm of professional mourners.

"You die. We cry." That was our motto. So whenever anyone passed away, we got the call to join the family and weep along with them. There was usually a bit of breast-beating and garment-tearing as well – anything to show how upset you were at the loss of your loved one. The rule was: the more upset you were, the more noise you made – and the more noise you made, the more you loved the one who died. So we got paid to make everything as noisy as possible.

Which is why I was surprised at the volume of the wailing that greeted me when I walked up to the office. Practices were never at full volume, so either one of our own had died or we were all getting the sack.

The minute I walked in, though, it all stopped. And six pairs of eyes looked at me.

"So where have you been?" moaned Martha, who actually was a "moaner". It's an important speciality – that sort of continuous, low-end thrum at the bottom of the grieving package.

"I was out of town. At my aunt's," I shrugged. "I just got back. Did I miss something?"

"MISS SOMETHING!" shrieked Shirley, who, true to her job description, forced me to put my fingers in my ears. "ONLY THE WORST THING THAT'S HAPPENED TO US IN YEARS!"

"It's that Jesus again," sighed Sarah, like the world was about to end.

"You mean the rabbi?" I asked.

"OF COURSE WE MEAN THE RABBI!"

shrieked Shirley. And a ceramic pot shattered somewhere on the far side of the room.

"It's all right, dear," whispered Sylvia, sympathetically, as she took my hand. "You're new. We understand." And there were tears in her eyes. But then, there were always tears in her eyes. That was her job. To be compassionate, understanding, and… well… sympathetic.

"She's only an apprentice," moaned Martha. "Nothing more than a sniffler. How could she possibly understand?"

Martha was right, of course. I was just a sniffler. But sniffling was where everyone started. And basic as it may be, it brought a depth to the occasion.

The watery eyes, the handkerchief, the runny nose, the little strand of snot. People appreciated it, I think. And I took pride in the contribution I made.

"So what's the matter with Jesus?" I sniffled, rubbing my nose with the back of my hand for effect. "As far as I've heard, he does good things. Making blind people see. Making lame people walk…"

"And making dead people alive again," sighed Sarah, as if that were the worst thing that could possibly happen.

"It started nearly three years ago!" wept Wilma, who seemed genuinely weepy. "Up in G..G..G…"

She was struggling to control herself.

"Galilee," said Sylvia, finishing the sentence and taking hold of Wilma's hand as a gesture of support.

"There was a widow whose boy died," moaned Martha, as if she was the widow herself. "And Jesus showed up during the funeral procession."

"He t..t..t..t..touched the casket," wept Wilma.

"And brought the boy back to life again," Sarah sighed.

"That sounds like a good thing," I suggested.

"THE WIDOW WANTED HER MONEY BACK!" shrieked Shirley. "OUR PEOPLE WERE THERE. THEY WEPT. THEY WAILED. THEY MOURNED. THEY SHOWED THE UTMOST PROFESSIONALISM. BUT BECAUSE THE BOY WAS ALIVE AGAIN, HIS MOTHER WANTED HER MONEY BACK!!"

"I see," I sniffled. And I really did. Shirley could be truly frightening. "So it's sort of about profit?" A low growl emanated from the far corner of the room. Anna had been quiet to this point. I'd forgotten she was there. But anger, they say, is one of the necessary stages of grief. And Anna could do "anger" like nobody else I knew.

"It's not about profit," she growled. And I have no idea how she managed to do that voice. It hardly sounded human. "It's about pride in one's work. It's about honouring one's position. It's about respect!"

"And if Jesus had just kept his nose out of it," moaned Martha, "then everything would have been all right."

I scratched my head, confused. "But the boy would have still been dead," I said.

Sylvia took hold of my hand, a single tear trickling down her cheek. "I can see how you might look at it that way, dear. But you have to consider the other outcomes. The widow was, indeed, given a refund, and as a result, our employer had to let a few of us go. We lost two eye-daubers and one of our best breast-beaters."

"A tragedy," sighed Sarah. "Truly a tragedy."

Wilma started weeping again. "And then… and then… and then… there was that business up in C..C..C..Capernaum." She blew her nose and, then, something ripped.

Personally, I've never understood garment-rending. Seems a waste of a perfectly decent dress. But I guess the point is that if you're upset enough to tear up something you paid good money for, then you're pretty upset. It's hard going, though, ripping up all that cloth, so Gomer, our chief garment-render, conserved as much energy as possible. Well, that's the official explanation. I just think she liked to nap. But she wasn't napping anymore.

"The dead girl was the daughter of Jairus." Riiiiiip!

"An official in the synagogue. Our people were there, just doing their job. When this Jesus shows up. And says she's only sleeping. I know a dead person when I see one. And so does everyone else who works for this firm. And so someone laughed at his suggestion." Riiiiiiip!

"NOOOOOOOOOOOO!" shrieked Shirley. "NOOOOOOOOOOOOOOOOOOOOOOOOOOOO!"

Everyone covered their ears and hit the floor. Pottery exploded across the room. And the dog clawed its way out the front door.

Shirley finally stopped. And passed out. Sylvia took my hand again (it was starting to creep me out). And now there were tears running down both cheeks. And a little blood trickling out of one ear. She might actually have been in pain.

"You understand the problem, dear? Do you?"

I nodded. "It's the prime directive, isn't it? The thing that must never, ever happen. A professional mourner. Laughing."

"That's right, dear," Sylvia replied, her grip a vice on my hand. "Sometimes family members will laugh. It's down to nervousness, mostly. But we must always, in every circumstance, maintain a sorrowful disposition. It's just good form. And I am afraid, on that occasion, that all semblance of proper decorum was lost."

"I blame the rabbi," Anna growled. And there was a great deal of nodding and moaning and sighing and ripping, etcetera, in reply.

"If he hadn't made such a ridiculous suggestion," she continued, "it would never have happened. And more good workers would not have been lost."

"They couldn't be trusted after that," moaned Martha.

"And the daughter?" I dared to ask.

"She lived," Sarah sighed. "So maybe she WAS just sleeping."

"Or maybe he brought her back from the dead," I suggested. "Like he did with the widow's son."

Wilma started weeping again. "The p..p..p..point is that he's not up in Galilee any longer. He's here, in B..B..B..Bethany. Just up the road!"

"And he's up to his old tricks," growled Anna.

"What? Raising people from the dead?" I asked.

"I'm afraid so," whispered Sylvia, wrapping her arm around my shoulder. "It's bad news, I know. But it has to be faced."

"But it's not…," I started to say.

"Not the end of the world, dear," said Sylvia, patting me on the head. "Yes, I'm certain of that. We all are. But we must be vigilant."

"The dead man's name was Lazarus," said Gomer with a riiiiiip!

"He was one of Jesus' friends," sighed Sarah. "And he was very ill."

"The man's sisters begged for Jesus to come," moaned Martha.

"But he stayed away and let his friend die," Anna growled.

"To be fair," added Sylvia, "they do say he stayed away so that he could demonstrate the power of God."

"In any case," said Gomer. Riiiiiip! "Lazarus was buried."

"They used another firm of mourners," Sarah sighed.

"The Dead Body Shop," moaned Martha.

"Amateurs," Anna growled.

And now Wilma was weeping again. "J..J..Jesus asked one of the sisters if she believed that she would see her brother again. The woman said, 'Yes, on the last day, when the dead are raised.' And then Jesus said the most t..t..terrifying thing."

"'I AM THE RESURRECTION AND THE LIFE!'" shrieked Shirley, popping up from the floor like she had popped up out of the grave.

" 'WHOEVER BELIEVES IN ME WILL LIVE, EVEN IF HE DIES. AND WHOEVER LIVES BY BELIEVING IN ME WILL NEVER DIE!' "

"Never die?" moaned Martha. "Don't you see? If no one ever dies, we're ruined!"

"And if people know their loved ones will live again," sighed Sarah, "and they'll see them, what's the point of grieving?"

" 'Cause they'll miss them in the meantime, surely," I argued.

"There wasn't much 'meantime' for Lazarus and his sisters," growled Anna. "Jesus saw to that!"

Gomer tore her dress with one long dramatic riiiiiip!

"He told them to roll the stone away from the front of Lazarus' tomb."

"They say the smell was overwhelming," moaned Martha.

"And then Jesus said the words," sighed Sarah.

"What words?" I asked.

Sylvia whispered it in my ear. " 'Lazarus, come out.' "

"AND HE DID!" shrieked Shirley. "HE WALKED OUT OF THE TOMB, ALIVE, ALL COVERED IN GRAVECLOTHES. HE DID! HE WAS ALIVE!"

And that's when it happened. That's when I

violated the prime directive. That's when I started to laugh.

"I'm sorry," I apologized. "I really am. I know you all find this news upsetting, but this is just about the best thing I have ever heard! An end to death? A future that lasts forever? Resurrection and life? I think I want some of that."

"Then you had better turn in your hankie," said Sylvia coldly, removing her arm from my shoulder and her hand from mine.

So I did. And as the room filled again with weeping and shrieking and ripping and sighing and moaning and growling, I walked out of the office and headed for home.

And I wondered. With this thing that Jesus was doing – resurrection and life – might there possibly be an opening for a Professional Laugher?

The Fussy Eater's Version

The Feeding of the Five Thousand

Samuel looked in his basket and sighed. Bread. Lots of bread. But no butter. And no jam.

And fish. Two fish. Flat and salted and hard.

Samuel was no fan of fish. And bread? Bread was not much better. But it was all his mum had packed.

So when lunchtime arrived, Samuel decided he would swap. First he went to his cousin, Anna. "I've got something amazing for my lunch!" he boasted, the basket behind his back. "Wanna swap?"

Anna rolled her eyes. "It's bread and fish, isn't it?" she said.

"Might be," Samuel answered.

"It's what your mum always gives you!" she replied. "You can't fool me. And no, I don't want to swap, because I didn't even bring lunch. My dad thought we'd be home by now."

"Oh," Samuel shrugged. "All right then, I'll ask someone else…

"Someone who doesn't know my mum," he promised himself. "Someone who doesn't know what's in my basket."

So off he went across the hillside, looking for a likely swapper.

He spotted his friend, Micah, but Micah's mum was the worst cook in their village. He'd gone to Micah's house for dinner once, and Micah's mum had served them this soup with bits of stuff floating in it. He thought it was chicken or maybe some kind of overcooked vegetable. But it wasn't. It was brain! Calf brain!

Samuel shuddered. He might not fancy fish. He might be tired of plain old ordinary bread. But there was no way he was going to trade it for a basket of brains!

Micah waved. Samuel waved back. Then he turned as quickly as he could and hurried off in the opposite direction.

"There has to be somebody with a better lunch than mine," he thought. And then he saw another boy from the village, Aaron.

Samuel didn't know Aaron all that well, but he'd heard that Aaron's mum was an amazing cook. It seemed like a good choice.

"Hey, Aaron!" he shouted, the basket behind his back again. "Want to swap lunches?"

Aaron, who was a bit older than Samuel and a great deal taller, folded his arms and looked down at him. "Well," he began, "you know that my mother is the finest cook in the village."

"Yeah, I heard that," Samuel nodded.

"Why, I remember the time we had the mayor over for a meal. Have you met the mayor?" Aaron asked.

"Yeah. Sure," replied Samuel. "Well, we haven't had him over to dinner, but –"

"I didn't think so," Aaron sighed, as if he was already bored with the conversation. But then he went on… "My mother prepared a lovely bit of lamb, marinated in red wine and her own special mixture of herbs…"

And on… "With barley bread… her own unique recipe…"

And on… "And at the end we had some beautiful fresh figs drizzled with honey…"

Samuel tried to get a word in, but it was hopeless. And he found himself in the strangest position – his mouth drooling, his brain turning to mush, and his feet desperate to carry him as far away as possible.

At last, he just swung the basket in front of Aaron and shouted, "Do you want to swap or not?"

Aaron peeped into the basket and turned up his nose. "You are joking, I hope? That food's not fit for human consumption!"

Samuel shouted again. "It's not drizzled with barley and fresh figs, if that's what you mean!" And he let his feet win the argument and take him to the other side of the hill.

"There must be somebody with something to swap," he muttered to nobody in particular.

But there wasn't. People were talking. People were moving about. Some of them were complaining. But nobody seemed to be eating.

So Samuel resigned himself to his fate, sat himself down, and reached into his basket.

Just then, someone sat down beside him. It was someone he didn't know. A young man, maybe eighteen or nineteen years old.

"My name's Andrew," said the man.

Samuel slowly withdrew his hand from the basket. "You don't want to swap, by any chance, do you?" he asked.

"Swap?" replied Andrew, surprised. "No. No. I don't have anything to swap with you!"

Samuel rolled his eyes. Another lost cause.

"What I did wonder, though – and this is going to sound strange," Andrew went on, "was if you

wouldn't mind coming with me and showing your lunch to Jesus?"

"Jesus?" Samuel shrugged. "The guy who's been doing all the talking?"

"Teaching. Yeah," Andrew nodded. "He's a rabbi – and that's what he does."

"And now he wants my lunch?"

"I told you it would sound strange," said Andrew. "Look, here he is. Jesus! Here's a boy. A boy with something to eat."

Jesus joined them. "Excellent!" he grinned. And then he turned to Samuel. "Would you mind," he asked, "if I borrowed your lunch for a bit?"

This was getting stranger still. And Samuel didn't mind saying so. "How do you borrow somebody's lunch?" he asked.

"Hand me the basket," Jesus smiled, "and I'll show you!"

Jesus shut his eyes and bowed his head. So did Andrew. And Samuel joined in – it seemed the polite thing to do.

Jesus thanked God for the fish. Jesus thanked God for the bread. Samuel was relieved that he didn't have to join in for that bit. He wasn't, to be perfectly honest, feeling very thankful.

And then, when all the thanking was over, Jesus reached into the basket and pulled out a piece of bread. He broke it in half. He broke it in quarters.

But the more he broke it, the more there seemed to be.

Samuel rubbed his eyes. Was this some sort of trick?

But no – the more Jesus broke, the more there was. And it was just the same with the fish.

Andrew and some of Jesus' other friends started passing the fish and bread around, and soon everybody on that hillside was eating fish and bread. Samuel shook his head. There must have been thousands of them!

When Jesus had finished and everyone had been fed, he handed the basket back to Samuel. There were still two fish and five pieces of bread inside.

"That's how you borrow somebody's lunch," Jesus whispered. "Thanks for playing along."

Samuel stood up slowly and staggered away, shocked and amazed by what he'd seen. So shocked, in fact, that he failed to watch where he was going and bumped straight into Aaron.

"Watch it!" Aaron grunted. And then he added, "Oh, it's you. Still carrying around that pathetic excuse for a lunch, are you? Well, I'll have you know that I have just had the most incredible meal. Fish and bread like you've never tasted. I'm dying to tell Mother about it."

And he rushed away.

Samuel thought about saying something. But what was the point? Aaron would never have believed it anyway.

"On the other hand," he thought, "if snooty Aaron thinks it's so great…"

And he tore off a piece of bread. And he took a bite of a piece of fish. And then he smiled at the miracle in his mouth.

For… it… was… delicious!

The Boring Version

Jesus and the Little Children

Nathan hated waiting. "It's hot," he moaned. "I'm bored," he groaned. "What are we doing here anyway?"

"If I have told you once," sighed his mum, "I have told you a hundred times. We are waiting to see Rabbi Jesus, so that he can ask for God's blessing on you."

"But I don't want to be blessed!" Nathan sighed back. "I want to go and play with my friends."

"That's the strangest thing I ever heard," grunted Aunt Rebecca, who was waiting with her twins right behind him. "Not wanting to be blessed!"

"So do you two want to be blessed?" Nathan asked the twins.

"Pickle," said Moses.

"Poo," giggled Jake.

"I'm taking that as a 'no'," said Nathan.

"They are two years old!" huffed Aunt Rebecca. "You can hardly expect them to understand."

"Well, I'm ten and I don't understand either," Nathan grumbled. "I mean, what good is it, being blessed? Does it make you cleverer? Does it make you happier? Does it make you richer?"

"It doesn't make you anything," his mum answered. "It's just a way of asking God to be with you – to take care of you. What's wrong with that?"

"Nothing, I guess," Nathan shrugged. "If it doesn't take all day!"

"We've only been here for an hour," sighed Aunt Rebecca. "That's hardly all day."

"Ducky," added Moses.

"Poo," giggled Jake.

Another hour went by, and Nathan spent most of that time on the ground, cracking one rock against another.

"We haven't even moved," he moaned. "There's nothing to do," he groaned. "Why is this taking so long?"

"It's kind of hard to tell," said Nathan's mum, standing on her tiptoes and craning her neck to see ahead. "There are a lot of ill people who come to see Jesus to be healed. Perhaps that's why it's taking so long."

"You'd think he'd do all the quick stuff first," Nathan grumbled. "A blessing here. A blessing there. Get it out of the way. And then get on with the harder things."

"I'm sure it doesn't work that way," huffed Aunt Rebecca.

"How do you know?" asked Nathan. "Have you ever seen Jesus heal anybody?"

"Well… no… not personally," she was huffing again. And puffing a bit, too. "But I just know – we have to take our turn. And you have to be a little more patient!"

"I've been very patient!" Nathan cried. "We've been here for two hours!"

"And we'll stay here until we see him!" she insisted. "You should take a lesson from the twins. They're not complaining."

Nathan rolled his eyes. "They're asleep!"

"Snn-rrr-fff," snuffled Moses.

"Poozzzzzz," snored Jake.

Another hour passed and still there was no movement.

Nathan lay on his back, perfectly still, staring into the sky.

"Get up!" grunted Aunt Rebecca. "You're embarrassing us!"

"But I'm paralysed," said Nathan through clenched teeth. "Can't you see I need help? Maybe someone will notice and they'll let us jump the queue."

"I'll do something if you don't get up!" his aunt threatened. "And then you really will need help."

"Mum!" cried Nathan, teeth still clenched. "Aunt Rebecca is being particularly hateful to a poor paralysed person who only wants a bit of a blessing and a miracle or two."

"It's not funny, Nathan," his mum sighed. "And it's nothing to joke about. Get up."

"All right," he moaned, sitting up. "Hey, look, I'm healed!"

"Very amusing," huffed Aunt Rebecca.

Moses sat there quietly.

But Jake had lots to say. "Poo", mostly. And "Poo".

Sometime in the middle of hour number four, the queue began to move.

"At last!" shouted Nathan. "We get blessed and then we go home! Finally!"

"That's what it looks like," said his mum, craning her neck again. "Jesus' helpers seem to be making two queues. One for people who have children. And one for those who don't."

"What did I tell you?" Nathan grinned. "They're gonna do us first and then get on with the hard cases. One of those helpers must have been listening to me."

Aunt Rebecca shook her head. "You really do have a high opinion of yourself, don't you, young man? As if Jesus' helpers would take advice from you! Why, that's just a load of…"

"Puppies," said Moses.

And Jake? Jake was nowhere to be found.

"Where did he go?" cried Aunt Rebecca. "He was here – I saw him just a minute ago!"

"Don't worry, Aunt!" Nathan replied. "He can't have gone far. I'll find him."

And off he disappeared into the crowd.

Nathan ducked and squirmed and wriggled through a maze of feet and legs and children. Lots of them looked like Jake from behind. But Nathan would not be fooled. And finally, he found his cousin right at the front.

"There you are!" he shouted.

And he was immediately shushed.

"Quiet!" said one of the waiting parents. "Jesus' helpers are about to tell us what to do."

"Go home." That's the first thing that Jesus' helpers said. And the second thing was even worse. "Jesus has more important things to do. He doesn't have time for all these children."

Everyone was shocked. And stunned into silence.

Everyone but Nathan.

"Go home?" he shouted. "GO HOME?? We've been standing in this queue for hours, bored out of our minds, waiting for just one little blessing. I'm not even sure what a blessing is, but I have waited and waited and waited for one and I am not going home until I get it!"

"Nathan!" called his mother, bursting through the crowd. "Nathan, it's not your place to speak. Be quiet!"

"That's right!" added Aunt Rebecca. "BE QUIET!" And then she looked around the angry crowd.

"He's not MY son, mind you," she added.

"But he's right!" someone shouted.

"It's not him we're angry at!" shouted someone else.

"It's them!" shouted several people at once. And they were pointing at Jesus' helpers.

"And so you should be," came another

voice. Jesus' voice. And it was angry, too.

"I don't know what you were thinking!" he said to his helpers. And he picked up Jake and handed him to one of them. "Children are trusting and loving and innocent. They are exactly the kind of people I want in the new world I'm making. In fact, if you want to follow me, you need to become just like them – not chase them away. Let the children come to me, that's what I say."

And the crowd gave a cheer.

Then Jesus put his hand on Nathan's head and prayed for him.

"Thanks," Nathan smiled. "I'm still not sure what a blessing is, but I'm glad you gave me one. And I'm even more glad that you told off those helpers of yours. The one holding Jake in his arms looks as if he really learned his lesson."

"He does look upset," Jesus nodded.

"And maybe just a little disgusted," observed Nathan's mum.

"Oh yeah, can you smell…?" added Nathan.

And that's when Aunt Rebecca cringed and cried, "Jakey, no!"

And Jake? Jake just giggled.

"Poo."

The Biting Version

Zacchaeus the Tax Collector

"Life is full of surprises." That's what my dad always says. "You can never really tell what's going to happen next."

So there we were, waiting on the side of the street. Stacked up, five-deep. Me and my brother Isaac and just about everybody else in Jericho.

I couldn't see a thing, to be honest. Abraham, the fattest man in town, stood right in front of me. And the fact that he was a fishmonger meant that he was also the smelliest man in town. It was not a good combination.

"Let's move," I whispered to Isaac. And then somebody bumped up behind us. I say "bumped". It was more like a push, like a shove. So I turned around to shout, "Hey, watch it!" or something like that. And – surprise! – I found myself face to face with one mean, scary little man. And I do mean "little". I'm only twelve, and I had a good five centimetres on him.

He didn't say a word. He just scowled and backed up out of the crowd and disappeared somewhere down the queue.

"You know who that is, don't you?" Isaac asked. "That's Zacchaeus, the tax collector."

"Are you sure?" I said.

"Positive," he nodded. "I was in the shop when he came around that time…"

"Oh yeah, that time," I nodded in reply. "The time his bully boys beat Dad senseless."

"I was hiding in the corner behind the big pots," Isaac remembered. "Dad kept saying that he'd paid his taxes already. And they kept saying that there had been a – what did they call it? – 'clerical error', and that he owed them even more."

"Rubbish!" I grumbled. "They just wanted more – and they reckoned they could scare him into handing it over."

"Well, he didn't," Isaac said. "He told them he'd paid what he owed and that was that. And that's

when they smashed things up. The pots, the bowls, and then Dad.

"And Zacchaeus – he didn't say a word. He just stood there with his arms folded, blank-faced, as if it didn't bother him at all. As if he'd seen it a million times before."

"I hate that guy!" I said.

"I hate him, too," Isaac agreed.

"So why don't we do something about it?" I suggested.

"Are you joking?" Isaac snorted. "His goons will have us for dinner."

"I didn't see any goons," I shrugged. "I think he was on his own."

"Now that you mention it," Isaac nodded, "neither did I. If they'd been there, they would have done the pushing and the shoving for him. He'd be standing at the front right now, with the best view in town."

"Which is also kind of weird," I said. "I mean, everybody is waiting for Jesus to arrive. Why would somebody like Zacchaeus even want to see Jesus?"

"Who knows?" Isaac replied. "Maybe rabbis pay taxes, too. Let's go!"

So we wriggled our way out of the crowd and ran down the back of the queue in the same direction the tax collector had gone, stopping every second or two to look for him.

We searched for what seemed like ages. The queue was huge. But then Isaac spotted him right at the end. And that's when it occurred to me that we might not be the only people in that crowd who would like to get their hands on Zacchaeus.

So I ducked back into the crowd, where the mean little crook couldn't see me, and jumped up and down, shouting, "Zacchaeus is here! Zacchaeus the tax collector. He's down at the end of the queue!"

"What?" grunted the man next to me.

"Sorry?" said another man. "What are you going on about, boy?"

"Zacchaeus! The tax collector! He's just down there. And he hasn't got his bodyguards with him!"

"Yeah, right," the first man scoffed. "He doesn't

go anywhere without his bodyguards."

"And what would he be doing here anyway?" added the second man. "Zacchaeus wouldn't be interested in anything Jesus had to say. And you can bet that Jesus wouldn't want to have anything to do with him!"

I was getting nowhere with those guys, so I popped back out of the crowd again, and there he was. Zacchaeus had his back to me and was heading for a tree. A sycamore tree, right where the queue of people ended. He was moving pretty fast. I wasn't really sure what I'd do if I caught him anyway. And then the strangest thing happened. Zacchaeus started climbing up the tree – like some evil, tax-collecting monkey. Surprise!

"Did you see that?" Isaac shouted, running back to meet me.

"Yeah," I sighed. "Now that he's up in that tree, there's no way anybody's going to get their hands on him."

"We'll just have to make sure he can't come down," Isaac grinned. "We'll make sure he stays there until the crowd thins out."

"And how are we going to do that?" I asked.

And Isaac just whistled.

"Bite!" I shouted. "Bite! Good boy! Where did you come from?"

"When I was looking for the tax collector," Isaac

explained, "I ran into Uncle Simon. He had Bite
with him and I told him I'd watch him for a bit.
I reckoned he would come in handy."

"And he has!" I smiled.

Bite was not the biggest dog in town. Not by a long shot. In fact, he was sort of a doggy version of Zacchaeus. Little and mean and horrible.

"If we stand at the bottom of the tree," I suggested, "and let Bite do his thing, I'm pretty sure we can keep the monkey-man up there until someone realizes where he is."

So we wandered over to the tree. Bite barked and snarled and leaped up against the trunk for all he was worth. It was perfect!

Then somebody shouted, "Jesus is coming!" and the crowd roared.

Some people were just cheering, but a lot of them were asking him to come to dinner, too. It was a real honour to have somebody famous eat at your house. I guessed he'd probably end up with the mayor or maybe one of the leaders at the synagogue.

I kept one eye on the crowd and one eye on Jesus, and Bite kept both eyes on the evil monkey-man in the tree. A closer look at Jesus, however, revealed that he was staring at the tree as well.

"Hello, Zacchaeus," he said.

And the crowd started buzzing. "Zacchaeus?"

"Zacchaeus!"

"What's he doing here?"

But the buzzing turned to a dead and stony silence (and even Bite stopped barking!) when Jesus spoke again. "I'm looking for a place to eat," he continued.

"I was thinking that your house might do."

The silence didn't last long. There was moaning and complaining and more swearing than I thought I'd ever hear at a "religious" event.

"It's an outrage!"

"Has Jesus gone mad?"

"Zacchaeus is the worst sinner in town!" the crowd howled.

And Bite howled, too. Until Uncle Simon appeared and dragged him away, embarrassed.

And Jesus? Jesus waited for the tax collector to climb down. Then he followed him home with half the crowd in tow, angry still, but also curious to see what would happen.

"So much for that plan," Isaac sighed.

"Yeah, it doesn't seem right. He beats up our dad, then he gets to eat with the most important visitor this town has ever had. I thought Jesus was a good guy."

"Maybe he has a dog, too," Isaac chuckled. "Hidden under those robes of his."

"That would be a surprise!" I grinned. "But I sort of doubt it. I wouldn't mind seeing what happens now. The crowd's pretty worked up. Let's watch."

So off we went. And then we waited. It took ages. But finally, Zacchaeus' front door opened, and he and Jesus came out (to more than a few boos).

"I have an announcement to make!" Zacchaeus shouted. "I have decided to give half of what I own to the poor."

That shut the crowd up.

"Furthermore, if I have cheated any of you, I will pay you back four times what I took."

Silence. Shock. And then the biggest cheer I have ever heard. And then Jesus spoke. "Salvation has come to this house today," he said. "And that is why I have come – to seek out and to save those who are lost."

There was another cheer, and then Zacchaeus began walking toward my brother and me. Had he seen us with Bite? Did he suspect anything? Would Jesus step in and save us, too?

"You're the potter's boys, aren't you?" he said.

"That's right," I answered nervously.

"That's us," added Isaac.

"Well, I cannot tell you how sorry I am for what happened to your father," he continued. "Or rather," correcting himself, "what I did to your father."

Then he held out a moneybag, and I swear I saw tears in his eyes.

"Please take this to him," he said, "with my most humble apologies and my assurances that nothing like that will ever happen again."

He put the bag in my hand, wiped his eyes, and then walked away.

"I didn't expect that," Isaac whispered.

"Me neither," I whispered back.

It's like my dad always says, I guess. Life is full of surprises.

The Nephew's Version

Judas Agrees to Betray Jesus

I turned the corner, and there he was, in the alley. My Uncle J!

"Uncle J!" I called. "Uncle J!"

He didn't turn around at first, so I kept calling. And finally, he whipped round with his finger to his mouth.

"Quiet, Simon!"

He used to be a revolutionary, my Uncle J. Part of this underground movement that wanted to overthrow the Romans and kick them out of our country. He had a really cool knife and everything, which he kept hidden under his robes. He'd sneak up behind a soldier or a Roman official maybe. He'd pull out that knife and *snick*, game over for the Roman! I wished he'd never left. I mean I couldn't tell my friends or anything, but to have an uncle who was sort of like a spy. Amazing!

"So are you murdering Romans again?" I whispered.

He shook his head. "No. There are just some people I need to… avoid." Then he pushed me away. "You should go home."

I was disappointed. "Is it because you're all religious now? Working for that Jesus?"

Uncle J sighed. "I don't work for him. I'm one of his disciples. It's like a training programme for rabbis…"

I just stared at him, blank-faced. Killing Roman soldiers was cool. Training to be a rabbi – not so much.

"Look, just go home!" he repeated.

And that's when the two men walked up behind him. I saw them first and thought they might be some of his old friends. They definitely looked like killers. They had big chests and big arms and big scars.

One of them grabbed Uncle J, slammed him against a wall, and put a knife to his throat. The other one put his hand around my neck. Really!

One hand! Right around my neck!

Not exactly friends, then.

"Listen up, Iscariot," the one with the knife growled. "We want the money. Now!"

"I haven't got it," said Uncle J. "I told your boss. He said he'd give me more time."

"He thought you were broke, Iscariot," the other one growled. "But we've been following you, and you've been spending a lot of money lately. Money that should have gone to him!"

"Don't be ridiculous," Uncle J replied. "I haven't spent a thing. I haven't had the time."

The first one pushed the knife closer. I could see a tiny drop of blood on the blade.

"Recognize the knife, Iscariot?" he sneered. "We took it as partial payment the last time you owed us money."

Uncle J forced a smile. "Well, you've kept it sharp. I'll give you credit for that."

"Credit?" the knife-man laughed. "That's the problem, isn't it, Iscariot? You. And credit."

Then he turned to the other man, the man with his hand around my neck. "Go on, tell him," he ordered. "Tell him what we've seen him buying on our boss's credit!"

"First day of the week," big-hand-man grunted. "You rented a donkey and its colt – just outside the city.

"Second day of the week, you paid a huge amount of money to the Temple authorities for wrecked tables and escaped doves.

"Third day of the week, you put a deposit on

a first floor room…"

"Wait! Wait!" my uncle interrupted. "None of those were my own expenses. Jesus wanted to enter the city on a donkey. He busted up a few things in the Temple. And he needs a room for the Passover. All of those expenses were for him!"

"His boss," I added. Though, with the man's hand around my throat, it came out kind of croaky.

"He's not my boss!" Uncle J sighed. "How many times do I have to tell you that?"

"But he lets you spend his money?" asked knife-man.

"It's all our money. Sort of. People give it to us. Rich women. Other supporters. And Jesus… well… Jesus more or less put me in charge of it."

Big-hand-man loosened his grip a bit, threw back his head, and roared with laughter.

"He put YOU in charge of the money? YOU? I thought this Jesus was some kind of prophet. He's gotta know better than that!"

"I don't know what he knows," Uncle J muttered. "But he is a second-chance kind of person, so maybe…"

"Maybe he still trusts you?" chuckled knife-man. "And you're telling us that you have never, shall we say, 'borrowed' from this fund of his?"

I looked at Uncle J. He looked at the ground.

"Yeah, well, maybe once or twice," he mumbled.

"But I can't do it again! I mean it. There's this other disciple, John. He's always watching now. I think he's on to me."

"Not our problem," knife-man replied. "But it is your problem. And if you don't come up with the goods by the first day of next week, this knife of yours is going to find its way back to its owner, in a not-very-pleasant manner. Do I make myself clear?"

Uncle J nodded. "Very clear."

"Then our business is done," said knife-man. "For the present, at least."

"Can I let go of the kid, now?" asked big-hand-man. "My fingers are cramping."

So the knife-man put his knife away. The other took his big mitt off my throat. And they walked away, down the street.

Uncle J stood there, silent. I rubbed my neck.

"So what are you going to do?" I asked, at last.

"I don't know! I don't know!" he shouted.
"I thought I told you to go home!"

"Sorry," I said. "I'm just trying to help."

"Well, you can't help, all right!" he was still
shouting. And then he hung his head and sighed.
"Unless, of course, you've got twenty-nine pieces of
silver on you."

"Whoa. That's a lot of money!" I replied.

"Worth killing a man for," he nodded. "I've seen
people die for far less."

And then, suddenly, there were two more men
standing behind Uncle J. But they were as different
from the first men as two sets of
people could be.

I looked up and coughed and
gestured.

Uncle J leaped to his feet,
fists clenched. "I told you I'd
get your money!"
he cried, turning
around. But
when he saw the
men, he stepped
back. He settled
down. And he
apologized.
"Sorry, I
thought you

were someone else."

"Apparently," one of the men smiled. "No harm done."

The other man looked at me. He was smiling, too.

"We're priests, young man. And we wondered if we could have a word with your friend?"

"Ahhh, more religious people," I thought. "Not nearly as interesting as the guys with the knives and big hands, but not nearly as dangerous, either."

That's what I thought. But all I said was, "He's my uncle, actually." And I smiled back.

"With your uncle, then," said the first priest. "It won't take long. We couldn't help but overhear and think we might have a way to help him with his problem."

Uncle J shrugged, gave me a puzzled look, and walked off with them. And in no time at all, he was back.

"So did it work?" I asked. "Are they gonna give you the money?"

"Yeah," he nodded, quietly.

"Amazing!" I shouted. "That's amazing!" And then I paused. "They don't want you to kill anybody or anything, do they?"

"Don't be ridiculous," he grunted. "I don't do that any more. You know that. No, they just want me to do them a favour. Introduce them to somebody. That's all. It should be fine."

"Introduce them to somebody? For twenty-nine pieces of silver?" I laughed. "That must be some special guy!"

"Yeah," he nodded again, more quietly still. "He is. And it's thirty pieces of silver, actually. I hope I've made the right choice."

"Are you kidding?" I said. "What a deal! You are the coolest guy ever, Uncle J. Spy. Rabbi. Wheeler-dealer. I want to be just like you when I grow up."

"Thanks kid," he muttered, as he turned to walk away. But maybe you'd be better off…" And then he stopped, mid-sentence.

"Never mind," he finished, as he waved goodbye. "See you around, kid."

And I waved back. "See you around, Uncle J."

The Neighbour's Version

Jesus is Put to Death on the Cross

I always looked up to my next-door neighbour,
Aaron.

He was older than me, by ten years. But if any
of the other kids started bullying me, he would
always be there, to tell them off or fight them off or
whatever.

I remember this time when Daniel, up the street,
was chasing me. I don't even remember why, but
he was bigger than me and it happened a lot. I
was almost home, almost safe, when I tripped and
fell face first in the dirt. And just as he was about

to jump on me and pound me, Aaron showed up, grabbed him by the collar, and hoisted him in the air.

"You want to mess with my neighbour?" he growled. "You'll have to mess with me first."

Then he dropped Daniel, who took off at once and didn't stop running until he'd reached the end of the street.

Aaron grinned and helped me up, and his mum asked me in and gave me a piece of a cake she'd been making. Then Aaron went off to work with a "You tell me if he gives you any more trouble" and another grin.

I always looked up to Aaron. So when my mum told me that he'd been arrested, it was a big shock.

"What do you mean?" I asked. "What did he do? They must have the wrong guy!"

But all she could do was cry and shake her head. And then, when she stopped crying, she said, "He stole. Stole from his boss. And you know what that means."

I did.

Aaron worked for a tax collector. He didn't actually collect the taxes. And he definitely wasn't one of those guys who went around breaking people's arms if they didn't pay. He did the accounts. That's all. He kept the books.

But because stealing from tax collectors was

pretty much the same as stealing from the Roman government, he was in really big trouble.

"That's just what they say, though, isn't it?" I asked my mum. "He didn't really do it, did he?"

She shook her head again. "Who knows? But if they arrested him, they must be pretty certain."

I pounded a fist into the palm of my hand. "I bet it was a set-up. I bet it was that tax collector he works for. He even *looks* evil."

"It doesn't matter," my mum shrugged. "The Romans will use this as an example to keep other people from stealing."

"But that's not fair!" I shouted. "Not if he didn't do it!"

"Life's not fair," she sighed. "It's not fair that the Romans occupy our country. It's not fair that our taxes pay for them to do it. It's not fair that their soldiers seize ordinary people and put them to work for nothing." And here her voice got really quiet. "And it's not fair that some of those people die in terrible accidents."

She was talking about my dad. Lots of conversations finished with him. And I can see why. If the soldiers hadn't grabbed him and forced him to load their supply wagon, then he wouldn't have been there, at the back, when the brakes let go and the wagon started rolling. And the wagon wouldn't have run him over.

Six years ago – that's when it happened. I was only five. And maybe that's why I always think of sadness when I think about my mum. And maybe that's why I looked up to Aaron.

He was always there for me, like the big brother I never had. And he was never sad. Ever.

People say that accountants are boring. Not Aaron. He cracked jokes and did these stupid magic tricks and was always bringing me surprises. It's like he was making up for my dad not being there. And he did a really good job of it.

And that's why it was even more shocking, a few days later, when my mum told me that the judge had found him guilty.

"I don't believe it!" I said. "They must have got something wrong."

Sadly, she shook her head. "No. I talked to his mum. Turns out that Aaron likes a bit of a flutter. He stole the money to pay off his gambling debts."

"So how long will he have to stay in prison?" I asked. And that's when the tears started again.

"Not long," she wept. "He's due to be executed. Tomorrow."

"For stealing?" I cried. "That's not fair!"

"How many times do I have to tell you?" she sighed. "Life's not fair."

"I want to see him, then!" I pleaded. "Just one more time."

"A crucifixion is no place for a child," she said. And she said it like she really meant it.

But I didn't feel like a child. Never have really. So I was going. I didn't care what she said.

Crucifixions in Jerusalem are always on the top of this hill they call 'The Skull'. It fits, I guess. Skulls and executions.

So that's where I headed, early next morning, once my mum had gone. I thought I'd have to be careful – so she wouldn't see me. But, for some reason, the streets were packed. So I just mingled in

with the crowd.

It was strange, really strange. Some people were laughing. Some were shouting. Others were crying like they'd lost their best friend.

"What's going on?" I said to a man as he pushed past me.

"Where have you been, boy?" the man grunted. "They tried Rabbi Jesus last night. Found him guilty, too."

"Guilty of what?" I asked.

"Blasphemy," grunted another man. "Apparently all those miracles have gone to his head. He says he's God. He says he wants to tear down the Temple."

"That's what they SAY he said!" a woman shouted angrily. "I don't believe a word of it. He healed my little girl. He was the nicest man I ever met!"

"They don't crucify Nice People," the man grunted back.

And I couldn't help thinking about Aaron. Okay, maybe he did steal from that tax collector. But he was always nice to me.

The crowd pushed and shoved its way up the hill. I couldn't see my mum. I couldn't see Aaron, either. But I saw someone else.

"Jesus!" some lady cried.

"Jesus!" spat some man.

And there he was – staggering up the hill, a wooden cross beam on his ripped-up back, a ring of thorns digging into his head. And there was blood; blood everywhere. I felt like I was going to be sick.

Then he stumbled. And he fell. And the soldiers grabbed this man out of the crowd and made him carry the cross beam instead.

When we got to the top of The Skull, they nailed the beam to another one, to make the shape of a cross. And then – I couldn't believe it – they nailed Jesus to the wood, as well!

The nails went through his wrists and his ankles,

and there was even more blood. And I couldn't
help thinking, were they doing this to Aaron, too,
somewhere else on this hill?

"It's not fair!" someone shouted. "He doesn't
deserve this."

And he didn't. No one did. Not to be treated like
that. My mum was right. Life's not fair.

And that's when she spotted me.

"What are you doing here?" she shouted.
"I told you to stay home!"

"But I had to come! I had to!" I replied. "I have to say goodbye to Aaron."

She fell to her knees then and folded herself into a ball and just cried and cried. I didn't know what to say. So I sort of crouched down beside her and put my arms around her neck.

"I'm sorry, Mum," I whispered. "I just want to see him. Please."

She stopped sobbing, at last, and wiped her eyes and pointed. "He's over there."

I walked slowly, really slowly, toward his cross. And the closer I got, the less sure I was that I wanted to be there. And then, there I was.

I'd always looked up to Aaron. And, sadly, I was looking up, now, as well.

His cross was standing next to Jesus'. But he hadn't been nailed like the rabbi – only tied to the beam. That was a relief. And there wasn't even much blood. Just bruises, mostly. But he was having trouble breathing. It was like he had to pull himself up to take a breath – and it looked like that was a really, really hard thing for him to do.

I didn't say anything. I didn't know what to say. And when his eyes caught mine, I wondered if I'd done the right thing coming after all. He looked so hurt and embarrassed.

"I'm… sorry," he struggled to say. "I'm… so… sorry."

And that's when I started to cry.

I wanted to be brave. I really did. But to see him there – Aaron, who'd been like a brother to me – and to know that I'd never see him again and always have to remember him like this. It was too much.

His mum put her arm around me. She was crying, too. My mum joined us. And we all just stood there – sad and pathetic and hopeless.

And then somebody started shouting.

"Jesus! Jesus!" came a voice from the cross on the other side of the rabbi. "You saved blind people. Deaf people. Lame people. Why don't you save yourself – and us with you?"

I looked at the man. His eyes were puffy and swollen and bruised. But I still recognized his evil face.

"That's the tax collector!" I said. "The one Aaron works for. But I thought…"

"They were in it together," Aaron's mum sighed. "They were both stealing – from the Romans."

And then Aaron spoke. It took him a while to find the breath. He pulled himself up slowly and he croaked back.

"Leave the rabbi alone. You and me – we deserve to be here. But he's done nothing wrong."

And then he looked at Jesus – looked him right in the eye – and said, "Remember me, please, when you get to someplace better."

And Jesus? Jesus looked right back at him and said, "Today. Today you will be with me – in Paradise."

And that's when Aaron smiled. Smiled like the times he'd told his favourite joke. Smiled like the times he'd played a trick on someone. Smiled like the times he'd showed up at the door with a surprise for me.

And I looked up at him and smiled back. And he winked. And he shut his eyes. And my mum took my hand and led me away. And I went with her gladly. And that's the last I saw of him.

It's been a couple of months now since Aaron

died. And Jerusalem has not stopped buzzing.

Not because of him. Or his boss. But because of Jesus.

They say he came back to life.

They say his friends saw him and talked to him and ate with him.

They say that he took them up a hill and that he just rose straight up into heaven.

I don't know what I think about any of that. But I hope it's true. Because if Jesus is in heaven, then Aaron is, too.

Life may not be fair. People still don't get what they deserve. But if that means, in Paradise, thieves get forgiveness instead of the punishment they deserve, then that's probably a good thing.

Must remember to mention that to Mum.

The Yawner's Version

Paul Performs a Miracle

"Mum," I said. "I'm tired. I've been working all day!"

"Mum," I said. "I don't like 'lectures' at the best of times. Give me something to do, yes, and I'm with you. But to just sit there and listen to some guy talking. It's not really my thing."

"Mum," I said. "I'm glad that this Jesus stuff you're into makes you happy. Everybody needs a hobby. I'm pleased that you found yours. But a guy coming back from the dead? That's a step or three too far for me. So you go. And don't worry.

I'll make myself some dinner."

I tried every excuse in the book. I really did. But your mum is your mum. And when she gives you that look like you're killing her because you won't do what she wants you to do, it's hard to say "no".

And that's how I found myself on the third floor of some meeting hall in the middle of Troas. Sitting on a windowsill. As far back and as far away from the speaker as I could get.

Mum was up front. Of course! With a bunch of her friends, yapping and gabbing like she hadn't seen them for months. Except she sees them every week. And sometimes in the middle of the week, too. They keep her busy. And that's a good thing, I guess.

Like I said, they were yapping, but when the lecture started, they shut right up, and leaned forward, like it was some god or some hero that was talking.

Their fascination with the guy escaped me at first. He was a bit of a runt, to be honest, with a lazy eye and a tendency to talk without taking a breath. But he seemed sincere enough, like he really believed in what he was saying. I'd go so far as to say that he was passionate about it — and obviously wanted the rest of us to be passionate, too.

He started with the same story I'd heard from my mum. About this Jewish teacher called Jesus, who lived in Judea back when Tiberius was the emperor. He was supposed to be some long-awaited saviour of the Jews. He taught people about God. He did miracles. But then he upset some of the leaders and he was put to death. End of story.

Except that this Paul, who was speaking, said that wasn't actually the end of the story. He said that this Jesus didn't stay dead – that he came back to life after three days, and then went up into heaven. As I say, more than a bit of a stretch from my point of view.

But then he said something that really did get my attention. He said that he had actually seen this Jesus, after he came back from the dead! He had been an enemy of Jesus' followers and was chasing them and arresting them, and was on this trip to Damascus, when Jesus appeared to him in a vision or something and talked to him. And after that, he became a follower of Jesus, himself, and travelled around the world, telling people about him.

I made a mental note to try and talk to him about that when he was done speaking. Did he really see this Jesus, or was it some kind of hallucination thing – just his imagination? There was supposed to be some kind of meal afterwards, so I thought there might be a chance to get him off to one side.

The problem was, once he'd finished with the story bit, he just kept talking. And I have to say, it

wasn't as interesting. My mum looked like she was still listening. She was leaning forward and all. But she'd been part of this group for a little while and understood more of what was going on. And she hadn't been working all day.

I, on the other hand, had been up with the sun, and had been down loading and unloading boats at the dock. My uncle – my mum's brother – got me the job. And even though it was hard, it kept us going, which we needed, since my dad was dead.

I thought about other stuff at first. About the job. About going fishing. About what we were having for dinner. I was starving!

But the guy just kept talking!

I thought about sneaking out, but every ten minutes or so, my mum would look back at me and smile. No chance to escape, then.

Then I looked out the window. It was a long way down, but I could pick out the people walking past – what they were wearing, what they were doing. I started to count them, but that was probably the worst thing I could have done. Okay, they weren't sheep, but they might as well have been. Because the more I counted, the sleepier I got.

It was just a yawn or two at first, but then I couldn't stop doing it. So I watched the speaker guy again, but I had no idea what he was talking about by this time.

Mum smiled again. I smiled back. And then my eyes snapped shut. I was asleep, but just for a second. Or that's what it felt like. What time was it?

And then, you know how it is — the harder you try to stay awake, the harder it is to actually do it. The eyes kept closing, the guy's voice kept fading. And then I'd force myself awake again. And then the whole thing would repeat itself.

I pinched my leg a couple of times, I shifted my bottom, I did everything I could think of. And then I thought, what did it matter? If my mum asked me what I thought, I could always say I liked the first part and leave it at that. I didn't need to stay awake. So I gave in. I fell asleep.

And that's when I started to dream. Nice dreams at first. I was out on the boat with my uncle. I was fishing. It was hot and sunny. The water was reflecting off the sea. Then I was eating. Better still. This lamb roast my mum makes. Delicious.

But then, someone was chasing me. Don't know who. I was running. I was trying to get away. So I climbed up these steps. Up and up and up. I was on a roof. He was after me. Couldn't see his face. It was dark. I was scared. I ran to the edge of the roof. I tripped. And like happens in dreams all the time, I started to fall.

They say that if you fall in a dream and hit the ground and die, that you die in real life. Which I always thought was ridiculous. But that doesn't stop you from not wanting to hit the ground in your dream. So I did what everybody does when they're falling in their dream. I forced myself awake. And, much to my surprise, what I discovered was that I actually was falling! The ground was rushing toward me, but there was no waking up this time. Only darkness, as my head hit the street below.

And that should have been it. End of story.

But then I heard my name.

"Eutychus."

Off in the distance. But my name, nonetheless.

And when I had forced one eye open, like waking from a dream, there was another eye peering into it. A lazy eye.

And then somebody said, "He's alive!" And somebody cheered and somebody cried and several somebodies picked me up and carried me back up into the room. Somebody grabbed my hand, too. But I knew who that was. No need for guessing there.

"Sorry, Mum," I whispered. "I fell asleep. I fell out the window. I thought I was going to die."

"What do you mean, 'thought'?" said one of the men who was carrying me. "You did die, boy! And Paul brought you back to life again!"

"Hush!" said my mum. "There's no need to go into it – not yet. Let him get his strength back first!"

"But it's a miracle!" said one of the other men. "Everybody ought to know!"

"All in good time," said my mum. And she squeezed my hand again. "I'm just so glad that you're all right," she sniffled.

"Me, too," I groaned. "Me, too."

So they laid me down upstairs and everybody had this meal that they call the eucharist, which means "thanks", which seemed particularly appropriate that night, especially for me and my mum.

I never did get to talk to that Paul about him seeing Jesus. I thanked him, of course – more thanks – but it didn't seem right, somehow, to question whether he'd talked to a man who'd come back from the dead – seeing as he'd sort of helped me do that, too.

And that's my little tale, I guess.

I listened to a talk by a man called Paul. It went on a bit long. I fell asleep. I fell three storeys out of a window. End of story.

Not!

Also by Bob Hartman

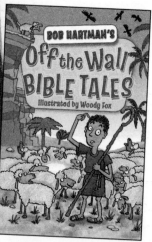

Look out for Bob Hartman's stories in ebook